Yesterday Makers

A Story from a Time Machine

Russell Kightley

Yesterday Makers
A Story from a Time Machine
First published electronically by Russell Kightley
Canberra 2016

ISBN: 978-0-9943704-5-7 Paperback Edition 2017
Version 1.43

(Incorporates a modified version of **Pierce My Bubble**, which was originally published as a stand-alone short story—ISBN: 978-0-9943704-6-4—released in 2015)

Cover Art
© Russell Kightley
Front cover: **Atomic Brain**, represents the flaring of consciousness. Back cover: **Qualia's Jungle** (detail) represents powerful sensory experiences. *Qualia's Jungle* won the E. G. Harvey Award, Australian SF Art, 2016.

Acknowledgements

Thank you to my wife Lilia for her endless support and helpful comments. And for stepping into an alternate universe.

And to Phill Berrie for all his help.

CONTENTS

Opening the Book

Warm breezes blew in and played across Qualia's face, carrying unsmelt perfumes, and unheard insect drones. Beyond the arched and open windows of her cliff-top castle, an unblue ocean slept. And above its waves, a great and glassy ship, like a vast and upturned greenhouse, sailed by with sightless eyes.

She picked up a book—or what passed for a book in her time—and began to read.

PART ONE

PIERCE MY BUBBLE

Old Bedroom

I climbed down the gangway and into my old bedroom. It looked good. The books were there, dusty on sagging shelves, just as I remembered them. The bed was unmade. And my old lizard, a caramel-coloured *Cordylus cataphractus,* sunned himself under a bulb. He eyed me warily, then he slid off his rock and pushed his nose to the glass. He recognised me, even though I had changed so much. I was now an engineer, not an aspiring zookeeper— and far older and richer than I ever expected to be.

I looked back at the metal gangway as it wavered and cut through the translucent zone of wallpaper. It was forged from an exotic alloy—one that could survive the Boundary —and it led to my ship, which hovered outside, parked in an invisible siding in a different space.

I wanted to explore, but I only had five minutes—any longer and I could be trapped. And I wanted to survive. I wanted to visit other times—and a minute had already gone. I tore from my bedroom and raced down the carpeted stairs—echoing a childhood nightmare—and stopped by the yellow front door, its paint bright and fresh. The church opposite rippled through the frosted glass, and I wanted to check that it was properly built. I opened the door, walked across the small front garden, grabbed the creosoted gate—rickety even in this time—flipped the latch, and stepped onto the pavement. A car—angular and small, and long since crushed—chugged by, spewing thin fumes. Its driver—old and hunched and smoking, and long since dead—stared straight ahead.

I looked at the church, and I concentrated very hard, because the brain always plays tricks and fills in details that might not be there. I counted the individual courses for the height of an arched window. Valuable time, I admit, but time well spent. There was no skimping in the rendering, no artistic suggestion—the building was carefully drawn, not lightly sketched. Every stone and brick was there. This place was real.

A man and his Scottie dog walked along on the other side of the road, by the church railings. They both looked up, and the man smiled: if this were the real past that would have been enough to tear up history and destroy my time machine. But there was no history extending out from this place, for this was a bubble world: a place with no future—and very little past. And I had very little time here.

I ran back inside and down the hallway—past the hanging coats—through the breakfast room, and into the tiny kitchen. Fred, my old springer spaniel, stirred in his lobby beyond the kitchen door. This was his territory—a little room of brick and tile that led to the garden. I pictured his wicker basket, his tartan rugs, his toys, and his water bowl. And I remembered listening to him whimper as he slept there—for the lobby lay directly beneath my bedroom, and the sounds of his dreams rose through the floorboards and comforted the teenage me. And as I lay in my bed all those years ago, I had imagined myself to be a stone knight on a slab, with a hound at my feet—a strong man, eternally protected by his dog. Then Fred died, as dogs always do, but his whimpers remained. They were real sounds, and they came from under my room—as if he lingered to guard me longer. But his grizzling grew less frequent, and after a year he had gone.

He scratched at the door—breaking my reverie—and I let him in.

"Hello, Fred!" I held his furry head and ruffled his ears, and his whole body squirmed with pleasure. Every wiry hair, brown and white, was there. His damp nose wiped against my hand, his dark eyes drew me in, and I felt his soul. Time was ticking, but my dog was back from the dead —and I wanted to connect. "Let's go into the garden," I said.

He shot back into the lobby, spilt his water, and thumped against the back door. I pushed the handle, and he flew out—a cannonball of love and stupidity—and bounded onto the tiny lawn.

I stood in my old back garden while he ran circles round me. I looked at the stunted bushes and at the beginnings of what would eventually become a large tree, and then I headed back into the house. I left Fred in the garden. The last time I saw him, he was sniffing along the flower bed—a parallel dog sniffing parallel scents.

There were dirty dishes in the sink, and I hurried by with a pang of guilt and headed back down the corridor. I risked a quick look into the living room. The wooden elephant was on the mantelpiece; he had always been there, plodding across his tiled savannah to the clock. I walked over and picked him up. He was heavy and smooth, and unwilling to leave.

The front door clicked open, and there was a humming and bustling in the corridor. My mother was back from the local shops. I froze, hoping that she'd go straight to the kitchen, knowing she would not. She filled the living room doorway, blocking my exit. Her brow creased, her jaw fell open, and her bag thudded down.

"Who are you, and what are you doing here?" she asked. Her voice was remarkably firm, considering there was a stranger in her house and by her hearth. Her head tilted a fraction and her lips pursed, as if she were trying to place me. Behind her eyes, rheumy even then, her mind raced.

"No one, nothing, I'm not doing anything. I'm just…"

"Please leave." She moved aside to let me out.

I slipped past. "Don't worry, I'd never hurt you." And saying this triggered a memory of a story that my real mother had told me about a break-in, when two men had forced a window and taken her jewellery. She had met them in the breakfast room, and they had excused themselves. "We're leaving now," they had said. There was no threat, and no violence. And all this would happen thirty years in the future—not that this place had a future.

I raced up the stairs, stopped on the landing, and looked back. My mother held the hallway phone with her left hand and dialled with her right. Nine—her finger shook. The dial ran back, clicking like a timer. Another nine; she was calling the police, but they would never come—there would be no sirens or slamming doors, and no arrest of a time-travelling son. The police, and their station, and the shops around the corner, and the man with his Scottie dog, and the church that formed his backdrop, and my dog in his garden, would vanish in moments. But her call still hurt. It felt like a betrayal, but I had betrayed them. I had called them up: Mum, the man and his dog, my dog, the hunched and puffing motorist, the woman who, in moments, would take my mother's call, the policeman briefly at his desk, and the shopkeeper who had filled her thudding bag. They all thought it was a normal day.

I continued to my room, gripping the elephant like a weapon. The gangway was fading fast, and I climbed up—

my guts tugged by nostalgia and guilt—and back into my
ship.

Time Ship

The alloy walkway retracted with a neat thunk. The portal shrank, closing across the veil of patterned wallpaper, and shut with a click.

The ship was deep and dusty and dim, and as vast as a nighttime warehouse. But lights twinkled, and heaters glowed, and the great vault of its hull was stuffed with memories: books, and fireplaces, and toys, and bureaux, and table lamps, and easy chairs. There were cars—showroom-new and glinting—and bikes, and balls, and saggy hats. And terrapins in tanks. And coats on hooks. And oils of woodland scenes, and golden rings, and mirrors, and pens, and broken fossils. And a brass microscope, and scattered slides. They all looked real, but they were not. The ship had made them all, and its interface engines hummed beneath my feet, like distant turbines.

I ran a finger down a shelf and tapped the spine of a favourite book. I pulled it out, blew away the dust, and coughed. I opened it and saw my name in blue ink, written in the laboured copperplate of youth. The ship had been thorough in its copying, and had missed nothing.

I walked down the wall of fireplaces, to the one with the wooden elephant and the carriage clock. The elephant and clock were inherited and real, but they sat happily on the ship-generated mantelpiece. I added the stolen bubble-elephant. Now, two elephants faced the clock, and I walked away, pleased with the symmetry.

I swiped and tapped the wall, and little boxes lit and danced beneath its surface. Another portal opened, another gangway telescoped out, and I stepped back into my own world—and my own time—and into the arms of Acantha. She gave me a dry kiss and pushed me back.

"Well, how did it go?" She looked me up and down—as if I might show signs of a struggle—and picked a brown hair from my trousers. She reminded me of a woodland creature, in her colouring and fast delicate movements.

"Smoothly. The world was perfect—impossible to tell from reality. I'm impressed."

She pursed her lips and frowned. "It *is* reality. It's not a simulation, you know that." She shook her head. "How far did you get?"

"Onto the street, and into the back garden. I played with Fred, then I left him outside and came back. It makes me ache just thinking about it."

"I can imagine." She stared into the distance. "What about the sky?"

"The sky looked fine."

"No clouds?"

"I didn't notice. I'm sorry," I said.

"Did the sky change?"

God, she could be persistent. "I told you, I didn't notice the sky. I didn't notice if there were clouds. I didn't notice if the sky was pink or green or perfect polished cerulean. I didn't look at the fucking sky, not once."

"Was it raining?"

"No, I'd have noticed that."

She grinned. "Mmm, I'm not so sure. Your powers of observation are not that good…"

"I counted stones on a church, and I stroked dog fur. I *did* observe."

"I told you to check the sky. I need to know about the sky. Aart said—"

"I can always go back…" I taunted.

"Too dangerous. You can puncture a bubble world once, and only once. Do it twice, and it could explode. And the shock could reach all the way back here."

"It *might* explode," I said. "Only might. No one knows. Not even the esteemed Dr Aart Gourley knows that. It's all just theory."

Acantha grinned. "You want to take that risk?"

"No," I conceded, "I do not."

"Remember that you don't belong in a bubble—you're a causal alien—so you'll destabilise it, and a punctured bubble hangs in the void like a sea mine, ready to detonate if touched. *So leave well alone.*"

"OK, OK, I get the point. There's no going back."

"Next time, watch the sky. Aart thinks that bubble-skies might change when their time runs out."

"You just said bubbles hang around…" I smirked.

"*Bubbles* remain, they're immortal. When you visit one —when you're inside a bubble world—you're forced to travel up its time-trunk. The longer you stay, the further you rise. Eventually, you reach the end of the bubble's history. It's like riding an unstoppable lift, you have to jump before it hits the ceiling. *You get one go. That's it.*"

I shivered. "The sky looked fine."

"Just as well."

Pizza & Beer

That night we ate at our favourite pizza restaurant. We were the only ones there, and its empty tables added drama, letting us focus on each other. Acantha ordered for me, since I always choose the same topping. It's my favourite, so there's no point changing, and it goes with my favourite beer. The beer comes in a dark brown bottle, and the label shows a galleon in full sail. Acantha chooses something different every time, until she has been through the entire menu. But I'm not that adventurous—at least not with food. Halfway through the meal, she broke the silence.

"Where to next, Pax?"

"That depends on how far back we can go. And what Aart wants to do. It's his call." I was stalling. I could not think of a single time that I wanted to visit—not off the cuff like that. Most people probably have a bucket list of temporal destinations, like ancient Rome, the dinosaurs, or Columbus setting sail. But I just wanted to examine my life, and the lives of my parents. I wanted to find the causes behind my history. To try things differently. To use the ship as a what-if machine. To play with my own archaeology, and to find out why things turned out as they did—why I got deflected from art and settled for engineering, and why I ended up test-piloting a time ship that fell into my lap.

I cradled the bottle and stared at the galleon sailing across its label. It wasn't Columbus's *Santa María*, but a far later warship with more sails and more guns—an altogether more powerful ship. I stood the bottle next to my plate.

Acantha leant forward. "We should try for a hundred years. What do you think?"

"So the *Titanic* is out of the question?"

"The *Titanic*," said Acantha, "is definitely out. You're unobservant, *and* unimaginative."

I poked my pizza. "I'm not unimaginative. I built a time ship. That takes imagination. You have to give me that."

"You *launched* a time ship, that's all. Actually, it launched itself. You just stood there while it flew at the wall, made a portal, and burrowed through brick." She grinned. "It made you jump, I remember that. Your face was a picture."

"I wasn't expecting it to do that. Anyway, it was *my* ship."

"Aart gave it to you."

"*He* got it from Pierce."

I ate the last of my pizza, drank the last of my beer, and stared out at the passersby. I thought about Aart. The man was a genius, and Acantha admired him too much—it was a mentor-student thing—but I knew that one day she would outgrow him. And I thought about Pierce and his connection to Aart. And who knew what. And who *built* what—if anyone built anything. And who got what from where. But none of it made sense.

She dabbed her mouth. "I'll get you another beer."

My eyes widened at the offer.

She looked down and smirked. "I'll drive. You've done enough for one day."

"Today is getting weirder by the minute." But I smiled. A beer was too good to pass up. She must be feeling guilty about saying that I lack imagination, when clearly I do not.

Cycling Back

That night I lay awake, staring at the crack of light at the top of my window. I was racked by guilt for frightening my bubble-world mother. She was only a copy of my real mother, but she was alive and able to suffer, and I remembered how her eyes had flashed with recognition when she had caught me in her lounge room. She had stood her ground and called the police. She was brave, my copy mother, I'll give her that.

The ship called me, and its siren song rang through my brain. *Come back,* it cooed, *and make things right.* My head was hollow, and achy, and metallic. This was the altitude sickness of night, the jet lag of time travel. It was a state of mind ill-suited for important decisions, but I made one anyway: I would go back and atone. But not to the same bubble, not after what Acantha had said about them exploding, I didn't want to atone *that* much.

I wriggled in my bed, all itchy and distressed. I imagined the bubble worlds poking into the void, like strange fruit jutting from the trunk of history. I pictured my visited bubble as a cloudy plastic ball, punctured and rotten and full of horrors. I imagined piercing it for the second time, and having it explode, blowing out bits of Mum and Fred like spores. I scratched and rolled over. Then I imagined a virgin bubble, freshly minted by the time ship, all bright and glassy and pristine, with its interior time trunk clearly visible. Yes, I'd go to a new bubble—made from a different time, and containing a different version of my mother—and hope that the karma would somehow filter across the void and make things right.

I switched on the bedside light, got up, and scratched all over. I picked up my loose top and saggy pants and got dressed. I squeezed into the gym shoes I'd dropped earlier. This was the stuff I always wore, but tonight it felt like a deliberate choice, like putting on armour.

I turned up the hallway thermostat to twenty degrees and switched on all the lights. I paced the house, going from room to room, shivering and twitching and trying to concentrate, trying to work out how to make things right. I ended up in the front room, where I ran my fingers down the spines of unread books. I wound the clock. I peered at the hunting prints—with their frozen hounds and twisted horses—and I stroked the antique maps. But nothing came to mind. I leant my forehead against the cold window and peered out at the dark street. A faraway motorbike laboured through its gears, and I smiled as an idea formed: I would go back to when my mother had been attacked in the street.

The mugger had ridden a pushbike and grabbed her handbag. He'd knocked her over and hurt her hip.

My jaw clenched. I needed a weapon, something innocent-looking—not a knife, maybe a tool. I paced again, pulling drawers and opening cabinets, but there was nothing. I grabbed the emergency torch and unlocked the back door. I walked onto the sun deck and shivered, watching my breath. The outdoor table and chairs were covered by a tarpaulin, and their shape was hulking and coffin-like. This was a daytime place, and it felt wrong to be here at night—and its wrongness thrilled me, making me shiver and twitch.

The trees beyond the lawn were dark, like the edge of a forest, and the little garden shed was lost in shadow. But the ship urged me on. *Go to the shed*, it whispered, *and look inside*.

I wrenched open the metal door and ran the light over three bikes and two lawnmowers, and over hanging rakes and spades and coils of wire. Over paint tins, and tubs crammed with wrecked brushes. Over oils, and hammers, and boxes of seeds, and then across a black tube on a shelf...

I bashed the door back, leant hard against it, and slid the bolt. And I strolled back to the deck—with its clump of furniture—torch in one hand, bicycle pump in the other. And shivered again.

I locked the back door, switched off the lights, and turned the heating down.

I stood in the spare room, bathed in the glow from the shimmering portal. The ship's song poured out as if, deep inside its hull, a party raged that was full of promise and opportunity. I took a deep breath and stepped through. As my head crossed the threshold, my mind cleared, and I realised that sirens should make you *leave* ships, not board them.

I tapped the ship's wall, and buried shapes lit up. I scraped and swiped, and flashing mandalas span and throbbed beneath the bronzy surface. Lines flipped and stretched and intersected, and numbers streamed. I gave a final tap. The great craft hummed and clunked. A hiss, and a new portal opened onto closed wooden doors. I had reached the inside of my mother's garage from fifteen years ago. The time field seeped from the ship and into the doors, turning their creosoted planks into icy ghost-wood. I squared my shoulders and pushed through. Timber and iron tingled and scratched through my body. And then I was outside, in the fresh air of a back alley of a new yesterday, in a new bubble.

It was early afternoon. Children were at school, and adults were at work. This was a quiet time for alleyways, so hopefully no one would walk by and see the portal yawning through the wood.

I held the pump in my right hand and slapped it against my left palm, like a schoolmaster testing a cane. It was perfect, and I was ready.

I walked forty metres down the cobbled lane—the ground was uneven, and stained, and pointed with moss, and tufted with grass—and I turned left. My mother was on the other side of the road, just passing the hairdresser's shop. She bustled along, unaware of things in her own time, and unaware of me. Her handbag was on her arm.

I checked for traffic, crossed, and followed, clutching the pump like a truncheon. I was panting and alert, and she was panting and oblivious—we made a fine pair.

She stopped at the newsagent's, bent forward, and peered through the window.

A rattle of chain, a hiss of tyres, and the gangly thief— too big for his bike—mounted the pavement. He was sallow, and pockmarked, with a sparse goatee, and a hard and vacant look. I lunged, thrusting the pump like a sword. It telescoped out, shot through his spinning spokes, and ripped from my hand. And in a beautiful ballet—imagined many times but never seen—the front wheel locked, the rear wheel lifted, and the lowlife—his face wide with bad teeth—flew off.

His arms shot forward, his head craned back, and he hit the blacktop with a crack and a thud.

"Ooh," said my mother. "Oh dear." It takes a lot to drag her from her reveries, and now she was fully in the moment. "Oh dear."

A man I hadn't noticed before ran towards us—towards *me*—his face was scrunched, and his lips were drawn back, and his fists were clenched. He was thickset and rough. Maybe he was the mugger's big brother or uncle, his pimp, or his dealer, or even his dad. "Call the police!" he screamed, and pointed a stubby finger at me. "Somebody grab that bastard."

I thought of Mum dialling 999, and how everyone I met called the cops. Then I ran into the road, and past a car. I tripped up a curb and dashed up an alley—past a motley of garage doors: pink and white and brown and black. I ran past metal and stained wood, and past new paint and old. The doors flew by, all different—all solid. There were no exits here—no mouths of time ships. There was only *one* escape hatch and *one* ship, and it was down another alley.

I stopped, gasping, hands on knees. A roller door on my right creaked. There was paint across its metal slats: crimson, and green, and electric blue. And the graffiti—a thin circle, cut by a fat line, and pierced by a curving arrow—was glossy and wet. A stencil lay propped against the door. A spray can rolled across the alley, stopped in the central gutter, and dribbled red. Paint misted the air, burning my eyes. but no spindly youth scrambled up a wall, and no bony hand rattled a gate. The alley was clear. No one, I thought, can run that fast, or paint that well.

The mugger's mate thudded towards me. "Stop," he yelled. "Stop, ye fucker."

I sucked in air and ran—a kid again, chased down this same alley by Simon, the thug from the big school. Simple Simon, we called him, and I wondered if this bulky bastard was Simon the man, bigger, more violent, and just as stupid. But dates are slippery and faces change.

And I ran—past broken gates and broken glass, past litter and weeds. My throat burned and my legs ached. My heart thumped, and pain hammered my back. A heart attack, I thought, I'll die here in the alley, clutching my chest, and beaten by an idiot.

And still he came. I reached the end of the alleyway, turned sharp left down a connecting lane, raced across an empty road, and slipped into my own alley. Simon's boots thumped down the street and back to the shops.

I'd shaken him, for a while at least. I leant against a wall, shut my eyes, and groaned. I remembered resting against these bricks as a kid—when I was a brave space soldier with a plastic ray-gun. But that was another life, in another universe.

I trudged down the cobbles and stopped outside my garage. The doors wavered, soaked into transparency by the leaking time field.

"You!" Simon stood at the shop end of the alley, hands on hips. He was only forty metres away, and I could see his chest rising and falling.

I raised a fist, uncurled a middle finger, and poked the sky. He puffed up—animal that he was—and charged. I gave him my other middle finger and grinned.

He was five metres away—nostrils flared and spittle dripping—before he roared. I shook my head and stepped through the portal. An itch of wood and scrape of metal, as timber, locks, a hook, and five nails, passed through me.

I sighed and turned to face the doors. Simon was outside, blurry and distorted, stamping and yelling and shaking his head. like something wild behind frosted glass. The portal began to close, hiding his head and feet, making me safe.

He punched through the shrinking disc of ghost-wood, and the portal hesitated, like lift doors detecting fingers. I thought it was a safety feature, but the ship was freezing time, framing the moment just for me. Simon's fat fist was trapped in a glassy mount, like a hunter's trophy. His body still writhed outside, caught in the dream-molasses of the leaking field. I nodded in appreciation. "Clever," I said, "very clever."

"Thanks," replied the ship. It unfroze the moment, and Simon's fist shot forward, the portal's rim snapped shut, and fist and forearm fell. The ship had given me a present, like a cat delivering a mouse.

I spewed harder than I thought possible, spraying the floor and Simon's severed limb. I gasped, my guts clenched, and more came up. The world became a tunnel. And at the tunnel's end, and brightly lit, the forearm twitched. Its middle digit—pallid, and fat, and sticky with spew—unfurled. He was giving me the finger—even now.

A thug to his finger tips, I thought, and it seemed witty, in the way that dream jokes do. The arm jerked like a lizard tail, and I was fourteen again, and my pet skink had jumped, leaving its tail—coiling like a cut worm—in my palm. I'd thrown the tail down the toilet and heaved.

I took a long breath—forcing myself back into the moment—and kicked. The arm was heavy, but it slid. And as it slid, it span, its fist rotating towards me, its finger still up. A chute opened in the ship's wall, like a cartoon mouse hole, and the arm fell in. A glug, a scrape, and a splash, then a roar like a cistern's flush.

The arm was gone, the floor was clean, and the hole was shut. The room was empty, and there was no hum. The interface engines were off.

I would keep this visit quiet, *very quiet*. I should never have gone, and never goaded Simon. He was back in the alley—if the bubble still ran—stomping and screaming and jerking, his stump spraying the garage doors, painting a circle of red, crossed by a line and sliced by an arrow.

I walked across the bronzy deck, through the portal, and back to my own time.

I stood in the spare room, still heaving. Then I stripped by the portal's glow, walked to the bedroom, glanced at the thin line of light above the curtains, and snuggled under the covers. I scrunched my eyes and saw a white arm tumble in the void. What the hell, I thought, would I say to Aart? And why was the ship sometimes crammed with memories, and sometimes empty?

Aart's Study

Aart Gourley stared at an open file. Pages were scattered everywhere. Paragraphs were scratched out, and notes were scribbled in margins. His pen hovered, ready to strike again.

He was sitting in his office. The room was decked out like a Victorian gentleman's study, complete with an antique globe, leather tomes, and hideous mounted birds. Aart once told me that a well-educated Victorian could master the known world. And that is how he saw himself. And how he dressed.

Aart refused to fly, and he rarely left the inner suburbs, but his mind roamed everywhere. His eyes scanned the world through a screen. He had spared no expense on this computer, and it was disguised as a blotter.

He had an etching of the *Great Eastern* behind his desk. This was the steamship that had laid a telegraph cable across the Atlantic. It was Aart's way of showing his preference for ships over planes, and ultimately for telecommunications over actual travel.

But despite his conceits, and his insistence on visiting the world through his office, Aart was smart—*really smart.* He looked up.

"Delighted you could come, *Paxton.*"

"Delighted to be here, *Aart.*" I shuffled about, annoyed at the way he said my name, as if it were somehow funny. He always did that—as if *his* name were serious. I stared at his bald head. Like his name, his pate was outrageous and unreal. I thought he polished it, but I could have been wrong—I've been wrong about a lot of things recently. Maybe Aart was the real thing, from glinting dome, to pointed shoe, to…

"We've reached a limit, Pax. A limit beyond which we cannot go."

Here it comes, I thought. I tried to deflect him with humour. "Limits are like that, Aart."

"What?"

"OK, I'm sorry, I…"

"What *are* you talking about?" He frowned.

"The second trip…"

He waved, dismissing the subject. Then he glared. "A hundred years! It's impossible to break the century barrier. Absolutely. Bloody. Impossible. It makes no sense." He thumped his notes. "We've hit a brick wall…"

"No *Titanic* then, not even a minute on the dock waving at the doomed vessel?"

Aart stood up and stretched. "Of course not. Acantha told me you'd mentioned the *Titanic*. Then she giggled." He frowned at me. *"She rarely giggles."*

"Life would be better if she giggled more." I shrugged. "Although she bought me a second beer last night."

"Then anything's possible." Aart smiled. "But back to the hundred-year limit. I've been playing with the settings in my simulator." He tapped his electric blotter. A small rectangle glowed pink as a data field activated. "It doesn't matter how I set the parameters, the destination always stops at a century."

"What happens when you type in, say, 300 years?"

"It resets to 100." Aart shrugged.

"And the power settings, what about those?" I asked.

"Watch." Aart swiped up the right-hand edge of the disguised screen, and a band of blue followed his fingers. He lifted his hand and the band shot back, as if spring-loaded. He pursed his lips. "Same thing, it flips back to a few percent. The interface won't accept high power levels —even though the ship's barely using any of its capacity." He cleared his throat. "And its capacity's huge. You must have found the same thing."

I shrugged. "I've only tried low settings, so I've never hit the limit." I wondered why I hadn't ramped things up. I had what amounted to the fastest car in the world, and all I'd done was tootle round the block. I only had to swipe a wider arc and tap another box… "Is your simulator playing up, or is it the ship itself?"

"The ship's got the power to go back millions of years. At least, that's what Pierce said when he gave it to me. So it's a mystery why I can't aim further than a century. And if *I* can't, *you* can't. As you know, the simulator's identical to the on-board controls."

I nodded, but Aart's simulator was different. The ship didn't have a blue power-slider, for a start. And I'd never entered numbers. In fact, the on-board controls and the simulator were completely different.

"Maybe Pierce was boasting about its power. Maybe he got it wrong. Maybe he misunderstood," I said.

Aart ignored me. "It just refuses to go. Like a skittish horse that won't race, it bridles at the possibilities."

"Did you want to try the ship's on-board controller? We could try going back in time together…"

Aart looked at me as if I'd lost my mind, and shook his head. "There's no point. It's a fault with the controls— wherever they are. They're impossible to override. Can't do it here, can't do it there." He looked up at me. "I checked with Pierce, and he concurred."

Only Aart would use a word like *concurred*. "So it's protecting us?" I asked. "Stopping the ship from overreaching?"

Aart continued, as if I hadn't spoken. "It doesn't make sense. I admit it gets harder to create bubbles the further back we go, but this hundred-year limit is sudden. It's something else entirely." He sniffed and stared at an imaginary horizon. "Maybe the ship really can't go back, even if it wanted to. Maybe it's not the controls. Maybe Pierce *was* lying..." He trembled, reddened, and started to pant.

"Tell me about the bubbles," I said, trying to calm him.

He ignored me. "Or maybe Pierce let slip a truth in an unguarded moment." His eyes widened and his nostrils flared. "Which means..."

I had to flip his switch, and activate his professor-mode. "Tell me about the bubbles again. Go back to basics. Maybe it'll help us think straight."

He nodded. "OK." He clasped his hands behind his back—his best pontificating pose—and strode about. He reminded me of a stork: spindly, pompous, and faintly ludicrous. He flexed at his pelvis, making himself even more bird-like.

"Bubbles bud from the trunk of history—they're little self-contained worlds that we pinch off. They remain attached to the trunk by a thin stem, but there's no communication—you can't travel back to the real history from a bubble. In fact, you can't reach the real history at all —*it would create too many paradoxes.*" He frowned, and I nodded for him to continue. "OK, when you're in a bubble, it feels like a complete universe—with a history stretching back billions of years, but it's not." He pivoted. "Visiting a bubble is like climbing in through the roof of a sealed library. You can't open the library doors and walk down the streets outside—that town, and the world beyond, is unreachable. But the books on the shelves describe the town, and the world, and its blocked history. There are so many books. Books on dinosaurs, and the Roman Empire, and the Great War. *Books on the Titanic.*"

I squirmed. "So the bubble has *copies* of relics—like printed books in a library—even if it has no history of its own. There may be *copies* of dinosaur fossils in a bubble—but no dinosaur ever lived there, because the bubble doesn't reach that far back."

"Precisely," said Aart. "A bubble is bounded. It's not an alternate timeline, or another version of history. It's a photocopy of a slice of time, stuck out on a limb. It's a dead end, a cul-de-sac, a blind alley. It does not persist up the ages." He opened his hands. *"That's why we call it a bubble."*

"And that's why I only had five minutes there?"

"Yes, that bubble—with its copy of your old bedroom, your lizard, your dog, and the world outside—might have had a year or more to run. But you could have reached its end-of-time in an hour—you could have slammed against its roof."

"Then what?"

Aart shook his head. "I dread to think. The logical problems horrify me." He tapped his screen. "Go back to the ship and try for a hundred years. If you *do* manage to get there, don't stay. Just take a quick look—no more than a minute—then come back."

"OK," I said, and I stood there waiting.

"Go!" he said. "I've got things to think about." He thumped his screen. "Bloody thing!"

Trying for a Century

My ship hummed, drenched in power. It felt canted, but it was not—the feeling came from teetering on the edge of now, stroking a distant yesterday, what Aart called *the spanning*. "It's a cross between vertigo, seasickness, and existential panic," he'd said. He was right—but how he knew was a mystery, since he refused to board the ship. I suppose that Pierce must have told him, and that made me wonder how Pierce knew.

My ship settled without shifting, and I knew that beyond its door was a yesterday from nearly a hundred years ago. Out in that world, my grandfather was only fifteen, my parents were unborn, and there was war—but there's always war. And I had gone as far back as I could, approaching Aart's limit. I had less than a minute in the past—just enough time to run down my gangway, sniff the air, wave at a bemused and long-dead person, and return.

I emerged into a playground full of children. Their eyes widened, their fingers pointed, and some of the braver ones waved. I waved back. A stooped and spindly schoolmaster approached, his face a fist of wrinkles, his cane slicing the air. The children ran, and I retreated, clanking up my metal stairs.

The master's overworked face mouthed at me through the shrinking doorway. The portal closed like a sphincter, pushing his nose back into his bubble world, and I gasped, thankful that the ship hadn't bitten it off.

The walls creaked, the ship settled, and the spanning was over.

I was back in my house, and I slumped into my winged armchair, and dust pumped out, making little dancing constellations. I was unsatisfied, like a cruise passenger rushed ashore near a fabulous city, only to be pushed back on board—glimpsing the docks but missing the sights. It is a measure of my selfishness that I felt cheated, when I should have sympathised with the people created in that short-lived bubble. Like the five-minute children in their five-minute school, and their vicious but short-lived master, with his beating cane that slashed the air—a whole world made so that I could be a speed-tourist in another century.

I was back in Aart's Victorian study. The old man stared into space and breathed deeply. "You made your century." It was a statement, not a question.

I nodded, pretending that it *was* a question, pretending that we were having a normal conversation. "Yes, for a while. The ship went as far as it could."

"It's all we can expect." His eyes watered, and he stared into space like a man betrayed, so I left.

Introducing Pierce

Pierce Temple was aptly named, as it turned out. He was annoyingly debonair. Somewhat under forty, with perfect skin, perfect teeth, and a silky beguiling voice. I thought him deeply exotic in name and appearance—and how right I was. But that was for later. I wanted to know what had upset Aart, and I thought that Pierce might know.

Pierce's front door was expensive, and solid, and understated. Just like him, just like his house, and his vintage car, and his nameless watch. I knocked, and the sound was rich and discreet, like a butler's cough. Eight-seconds and no footsteps later, he opened the door. He was either wearing slippers, or he had been standing there the whole time. I looked down at his feet and saw not slippers but suede shoes. It was impossible to tell where he'd been —and when.

"Come in, Paxton, come in," he said, and stood aside. "There's coffee on." His clipped and careful speech, his cravat, his languid air, and above all his timing, suggested that he had polished his life by endless rehearsal. Pierce had something of the actor about him, an easy and natural charisma.

I followed him into the kitchen. Vegetables were partly cut, spices were scattered, and a bunch of coriander waited for the knife. An ice-white grinder sat like a chess queen in a square of spilt pepper. A loaf lay gutted, showing its fluffiness. And the coffee boiled.

"Black?" he asked, raising an eyebrow.

"Yes, please." I took the mug, sipped the rich brew, and nodded. "Superb."

"Take a seat," he said, indicating a pair of kitchen stools. "It's my favourite bean—grown on a mountain in Africa. I grew the coriander in the garden. It's funny when you think about the origins of things, isn't it?"

I nodded again. I did a lot of nodding when Pierce was around. "The whole world meets in your kitchen."

"Nicely put, Paxton, nicely put. Now, what can I do for you?"

I shifted on the stool. "Why is Aart so upset?"

Pierce shrugged. "He knows too much." He slurped his coffee. "How's the ship?"

"It works like a dream. I went back forty-five years and patted my long-dead dog. And I brought back an ornament—a small wooden elephant."

Pierce grinned. "You set the ship's tolerance at what, fifteen percent?"

"Twenty, the full theoretical limit. The elephant was well under that." My ship would accept an additional sixteen kilos—it was like the luggage limit on an aeroplane. The craft was tuned to me—and my mass—but there had to be a margin of error. I could have suffered an illness in the bubble world and so lost weight, or I could have misplaced an item of clothing. I could have gorged on ancient pudding and grown heavier. Aart thought that five percent was enough. But I'm an engineer, and I like wide tolerances— and I wanted to sneak some souvenirs back.

"As usual, you play it safe, Paxton." Pierce pursed his lips and stared into the middle distance. My move.

"Then I went back a hundred years—but only for a minute. I landed in a school playground. Aart said a century was the absolute limit."

Pierce frowned, but he ignored the reference to the hundred-year barrier. "Why a school?"

"Er..." But I had no memory of setting the controls for a schoolyard.

Pierce leant forward—chin out, eyebrows raised, and hands open—probing for an answer.

I shrugged, like a lazy student facing his teacher. "The ship must have decided." It was a hasty lie, but as the words sank between us, I knew it was true.

Pierce put down his coffee and smiled. "Time ships are very smart. They have to be: creating and visiting bubbles is hard, and opening portals takes great skill—"

"Ships?" I asked.

Pierce stiffened. "*Theoretical* ships. I was talking in the abstract…" He stood up. "Let me know when you make another trip. And try not to annoy the locals."

My cheeks reddened. "You know about Simon?"

He nodded, and his hand twitched. "It's fine…"

"OK, thanks. I'll be off then…"

But Pierce didn't answer. He was lost in thought—staring out at his vegetable garden.

Aart's Exit

The next day I rang Aart, and I waited on the phone listening to the endless tone. I was about to hang up, when his secretary answered. She was heaving and sobbing and gasping.

"What's up?" I asked.

She composed herself. "Aart killed himself. They found him in his garage. That's all I know…"

I had a brief out-of-body experience and saw myself walking through the phantom-wood of my own garage doors, back in the bubble. And in a parallel play, I imagined Aart's ghost escaping through the solid doors of his garage, here in the real world. I pictured a coil of rope—hanging on a nail—and I wondered if Aart had hung himself. Or if he had a vehicle stowed in his garage—something hunched and glinting and powerful, the automotive equivalent of a time ship—and had used its fumes…

The phone disconnected.

I wondered if Aart's computer was still simulating my ship's control panel. I wondered if I would go into the past again. I wondered what an alien bicycle pump could do to a bubble world, and what a dead arm could do to the void. I wondered what I would have for lunch, and why my desk was such a mess. A thousand trivialities crowded in, doing their best to push out the horror, but the horror stayed, hovering just out of view, droning in the background like a machine that someone had forgotten to switch off.

I called Acantha and told her that I was taking her to lunch. I must have sounded different, because she agreed with no argument. It's funny what a tone of voice can do.

We stared at each other, our eyes damp. Acantha sipped her beer, but her food lay untouched. She toyed with her fork—twirling it and drawing air circles—as if she could unpick Aart's death and stitch our lives back together. I grabbed her hand.

"You can't change anything," I said, but she pulled free and carried on twirling.

The pub was quiet, since it was before midday. The only other customers were two pot-bellied men in cheap suits and wide ties. They rested on the bar, swigged lagers, and snuck covert glances at us. I tried to distract myself by imagining what they'd think if they knew who we were, what we'd done, and why we were here.

"Why would he do that?" she asked. "We'd just succeeded. The ship worked. He had everything to live for…"

I nodded, like I always do, but I had the oddest feeling that my mind was floating outside my head, tugging and bobbing, like a tethered balloon caught in a draught. "Eddies," I said.

"Eddy who?" she asked.

"No, *eddies*. Winds, zephyrs..." I waved, hoping to convey vague influences. "Breezes..."

"Don't get all poetic and maudlin on me," she said. She put down her fork and looked me in the eye. "Are you OK?"

I nodded.

Pierce's Exit

Pierce's front door was expensive, and solid, and understated. Just like him. Just like his furnishings, and his car, and his watch—a watch that glowed, and hummed like a faraway beehive.

I knocked, but there was no response. I put my ear to the wood, looked around, and then tried the handle. The door opened, oiled and silent, and I walked through Pierce's hallway and into his kitchen. There was no half-eaten bread, and no half-prepared meal. The pepper grinder was there—still like an icy chess piece—but the spilt pepper had gone. Every surface was clean and polished, and everything glinted. It was too neat—even for Pierce— and I knew that he'd gone. The emptiness of the house shrieked at me, bouncing off the walls like a mad aunt.

I walked into his library. A giant mahogany desk stood in the middle, and on its leather top was a blotter, and on the blotter was a letter. A fountain pen lay across the paper, as if Pierce had just finished writing and had stepped out through the French doors for a breath of garden air. This was his final flourish—stagey and obvious—and it gave me a twinge of hope that Aart was not really dead—that his suicide, like Pierce's exit, had been staged for my benefit: that all of this horror was a sick tapestry that I could unpick with Acantha's magic fork.

I picked up the note.

Burst My Bubble

I left Pierce's house. The door closed with a final thud and locked itself. I ran over the words in Pierce's note, and each one cut into my mind, slicing up everything I knew. I glanced at the sky. The high clouds looked plasticky, and the sunlight looked electric, and I remembered Acantha's question: "Did the sky change?"

I wondered if Pierce had his own Acantha, up there in his greater world. And I imagined Pierce telling this woman how the sky *had* started to change, and that he knew that it was time to leave. I wondered if Pierce had his own version of Aart, or if Pierce was solely responsible for creating this bubble world that I lived in. I wondered if Pierce was cruel or kind to let me know that I was nothing more than a human photocopy. I wondered if Pierce's ship had a bigger tolerance than mine—and whether he'd taken anyone with him.

Should I have done what Pierce had done? When I had visited my own past, I had lacked the time to write a letter, but I could have run to the man in the street and shaken his shoulder and screamed. But he would have stared at me and his dog would have yapped.

I remembered a dream from long ago. My family had changed into witches, and could not be trusted. I had leapt down the stairs—the entire flight, from top to bottom, in one go—and raced into the front garden, and I had stopped a passerby and begged him to wake me up. And I felt for Pierce: he had been here long enough to bond to Aart and Acantha and me—and he felt that he owed us an explanation. He must have given it careful consideration— weighed the pros and cons of telling us—and balanced insight with suffering.

Pierce had spent a year in this bubble. It was his creation—or one of them—but it was our entire world. And he had given Aart and Acantha and me the technology to do the same. We had created tiny bubbles in our limited past, and I had visited them. And briefly, we'd been gods.

I wondered how far in the future Pierce came from. His features were fine but were they more evolved? I wondered what the real Acantha and Aart were doing back in the main trunk of history—the history that had a future. And I wondered what I was doing there, with no Pierce and no time machine.

Our bubble was nearing the end of its hundred-year span. I thought of Aart and the weight of his knowledge— of his knowing the truth while Acantha and I were oblivious. And how that burden had proven too much for him.

47

That night I took Acantha out to dinner. It was a warm summer night, and we sat under the stars. We toasted Aart, and Pierce, and time travel, and love, and contingency.

Acantha forced a smile and ordered me a second beer. And I knew that she had realised this world was ending. We laughed at the unspoken joke, determined to enjoy life while we could—while our bubble remained.

PART TWO

THE NEXT LEVEL

Pierce's Office

Pierce leant back in his chair and sighed. He scanned the bridge of his ship, which was styled like a Victorian drawing room in memory of Aart. But instead of Aart's favourite etching of the *Great Eastern*, there was a framed photograph of the twin ocean liners, *Olympic* and *Titanic*. Pierce found the choice unsettling, and he wondered why the time ship had chosen a view of the two vessels lying parallel, rather than a more conventional picture of the *Titanic* steaming alone.

Duplication, he thought. Choosing the sister ships was a reference to copying, for time ships copied parts of history. That's how they made bubble worlds. That's how they worked. And it was a reference to split destinies, for the fates of the two liners were so different. The time ship was talking to him, prodding and goading and injecting messages into everyday things.

Pierce idly flicked the controller, and contemplated another bubble. But his passion for time travel had drained away. His belly ached from the loss of Aart and Acantha and Paxton. They were gone, fantastically alone and unreachable, and trapped in a closed bubble that hung in the great nothingness that lay outside the trunk of history. He would have liked to bring them back, but his ship's luggage allowance was fixed at twenty percent of his body weight—and Pierce was not a heavy man.

He levered himself up, grunted, glanced at the metal sisters, and left the bridge. He walked down a featureless corridor—for the ship's interface engines had given up with the passageway—and he passed through a sparkling portal, he opened a nondescript door in a forgettable terrace, and then he stepped into his world. He squinted at the faded sun, and trudged off.

Three streets later, he stood outside his mentor's house. The door was expensive, and solid, and understated. And the sound of Pierce's knock was rich and discreet, like a butler's cough. But the house felt empty, and Pierce pictured the library with its mahogany desk, and on that desk he imagined a letter from his mentor.

He had a key, but he walked away, shoulders hunched, unwilling to put his imagination to the test, scared of seeing his own oblivion crystallised in blue ink. But Pierce knew that it *would* happen, for there was a symmetry to things. There were always echoes and reflections, layers on layers. Pierce—cool, and debonair, and highly evolved—was shaking, for his world, such as it was, was about to end. He looked at the sky, but the blue had drained away, and in its place were plasticky clouds and watery sunlight. His mentor had gone, having said nothing. He was, he realised, an experiment that had ended.

Pierce's Toast

That night Pierce dined alone. It was warm, and he sat under the stars, at the best table in the best restaurant. There was no point skimping, not at this stage.

The waiter poured the last of the champagne and retreated. Pierce—impossibly and fantastically alone at the end of his world—raised his glass and swivelled its stem. He watched the bubbles rise and he toasted Aart and Acantha and Paxton.

There was a rattle—metal on metal—several metres behind him. His eyes widened, and the champagne glass froze in his hand. He stared at the bubbles, not daring to turn. There was a clanking, then an unseen footfall—leather on terracotta—and a slight, and very polite, clearing of an unseen throat. It was a soft reprieve, a whispered comfort, a mother's hush before bedtime.

"Mind if I join you?" said a voice that was impossibly urbane.

Pierce gulped and wiped his eye. "Claude, it's you."

"Perceptive as ever." The visitor put a hand on Pierce's shoulder—a gesture perfectly measured with no overtones of superiority. "I wouldn't miss this for the world."

"You're still the master of the apt phrase," said Pierce, and he sniffed, hoping that his face was dry, hoping that Claude would conclude that he, Pierce, was facing the end of his bubble world—and the recent loss of his friends— with perfect equanimity. Hoping that his languid pose, and his raised glass, and his excellent table—with its commanding view of a vast city that twinkled beneath a dome of stars—would signal a supreme detachment. That Claude would see a toast to the inevitable given by a jaded time traveller who had reached the end of his journey. Hoping all of that, but knowing it was not true.

"My ship," said Claude, "is set to a tolerance of two hundred percent."

"I'll take that as an invitation, then." Pierce turned around and regarded his mentor. "Unfortunately, my ship was more limited, and I had to leave my friends behind, I —" His throat knotted, strangling the words.

Claude pursed his lips, and rocked, and inclined his head. His suit was perfectly made and drew no attention. Indeed, Claude's whole appearance was tuned to make him forgettable. People who saw him remembered a symbol— and Claude the person would fade away—which is just the way he liked it.

But if you concentrated very hard—and if you looked past his elegance, where nothing stood out—you would see a slender man in his late forties. You would notice that his features were fine—finer even than Pierce's—and that his eyes were an icy green. And if you could bear to look into those eyes, you would see the glint of a fierce intellect. It was a light that Claude did his best to hide. Unless—and this happened quite often—he wanted to stare you down.

"Time is short," said Claude. "We should go." The metal walkway—extending to head height before disappearing into the invisible portal—wavered as if to underline the point.

"Time is always short," said Pierce, and he stood like an awkward wedding guest, "and the champagne's gone."

"Bring the glass," said Claude. "I have plenty more on board."

They walked up the steps and vanished. The ladder followed, ratcheting into the mid-air nothingness, and the portal closed with a tongue-click, sealing the bubble world forever.

The waiter watched impassively, like a madman's butler who was used to his master's foibles. He cleared his throat and went to the table. There was a stack of money. On top was a note, scrawled in blue ink: *Spend like there's no tomorrow*. But the waiter was a careful man and he would save his tip. He scanned the city lights. The warm breeze picked up, carrying the scents of garlic and wood smoke, and the sound of distant laughter. *Well*, he thought, *maybe one drink...*

Claude's Ship

Pierce turned to face what looked like the atrium of a grand house—complete with a domed skylight, and a sweeping staircase—and smiled at Claude. "So this is your ship?"

"No."

"Whose is it, then?"

"It's not a ship," said Claude, "it's a mansion in a micro-bubble. It connects *your* world to *my* ship. The front door leads back to your world. The back door leads to my ship."

"Literally, a halfway house?" said Pierce.

"Yes, it buffers my ship from your dying world—like a tyre on a jetty."

A roar and a lurch, like a small earthquake. The house squealed, and furniture slid. A joist cracked, and something crashed down the stairs, splintering in the hall. An urn shattered on tiles, and an umbrella shot across the floor.

"Let's go!" shouted Claude. "Now!"

They raced to the back door. Claude grabbed the handle and pulled. A curtain shimmered, blocking their way.

"It looks like a waterfall," said Pierce, and he poked the shimmer with his finger.

Behind them, the skylight exploded, raining glass on the stairs. Panelling ripped, and a moulded cherub fell, snapping its arm and smashing its lantern.

Claude rammed Pierce's back. "It's breaking up—move!"

Pierce tripped through the portal and vanished.

A pipe burst, spewing water across the tilted floor, flooding the house like a sinking ship. Claude took a last look—savouring the destruction—and jumped. The portal flashed shut behind him. And the staircase, which had never led anywhere, detonated.

Pierce shuddered and shook, like a dog climbing from a pond. But no droplets flew, for the boundary—despite its watery look—had been dry.

They stood on a path bordered by flower beds. A stone arch—the portal's frame—towered over them, but the gossamer curtain had gone, and leaves blew through what a moment ago had been a door to a bridge to another world.

The path was cracked and mossy, and it led to a glinting ornamental lake. A black swan slid across the water, like a toy pirate ship. Mallards squabbled at the water's edge, and a flock of sulphur-crested cockatoos screeched overhead.

"Welcome to my ship!"

Pierce cleared his throat. "You *built* this?"

Claude smiled thinly, but his head stayed still. A dodo waddled towards them.

"Are the birds real?" asked Pierce.

"Yes, I've collected them from all over. What do you think?"

"Clever." Pierce clenched his teeth. "Your ship's bigger than mine."

"Much bigger," said Claude, "by a factor of billions. It's a little world. And it has menageries, but no people, and I prefer it that way—present company excepted."

"Don't you get lonely?"

"I don't *live* in my ship, I retreat to it now and then. I live in a proper world—but it's a world gone mad. I come here to keep sane. And I visit other worlds—like I visited yours—and that helps a lot." He inhaled and surveyed his manufactured kingdom. "It's my cruise liner..."

Pierce sucked the scented air. "Mine was a mere yacht in comparison. And now it's gone—lost in a lost bubble." He shook his head. "My world was mad, too..."

"We'll go to my world, but I warn you, it's quite a walk." Claude marched up the sloping lawn and under the horse chestnut trees, and stopped at an empty road. He pointed at the detached houses on the far side. "Well, what do you think?"

"They look solid and comfortable, with nice windows and trimmed hedges. But why go to all that trouble?"

"It reminds me of a favourite street in a town I once knew." Claude smiled. "And it's a security system."

Pierce frowned. "How do you mean?"

"There are thousands of houses here in my ship, and each has many doors. Only I know which one opens onto my world…"

"Isn't your ship tuned to you? Mine was tuned to me."

"Yes, but all security systems can fail. It's just another precaution."

They crossed the road and rounded the corner house. The building was heavy—all brown bricks and stone-edged windows.

"That's a nice place, and it must have a good view of the park," observed Pierce.

Claude nodded. "I use the main bedroom as a study." He pointed at the side garages. "And I keep a small car in there, in case it rains."

"Don't you control the weather?"

"No, I leave that to the ship," said Claude.

Pierce frowned, but let it go.

They passed terraced houses on their left, and a low stone wall on their right. Beyond the wall was more parkland.

Pierce stopped. "Tennis courts. You've got everything!" He turned and stared at a corner house with a shady portico. "Even a dragon on a roof!"

"The tennis courts are deserted—and I can't play alone —and the dragon is a carved ridge tile. But thanks."

They continued in silence to the end of the park, crossed a junction, walked past a never-used factory, and skirted an empty shopping centre. They arrived at a primary school, and the cries and squeals of children floated over its high brick wall.

Pierce raised an eyebrow. "I thought we were alone."

"We are. They're just sound effects," said Claude. "Look through the gates, and you'll see an empty playground." He shuddered. "The sounds move like invisible children. I can't stand it. It's been doing it for days."

"Why not switch it off?" Pierce looked through the railings at the ghostly playtime. A non-existent ball thumped against a brick wall to whoops and cheers. A girl giggled, and chalk scraped on blacktop.

"I can't stop it," said Claude. "It's the ship's idea of a joke."

"Strange sense of humour—even for a time ship. Perhaps it's trying to tell you something. Have you tried asking it?"

But Claude had hurried on, staring straight ahead. Pierce looked back. The chalk had drawn a circle, crossed by a line, and punctured by a curving arrow.

"Play with us, Pierce," cried the voices. "Jump in the circle." The tone changed, becoming deep and imperative, as if the ghost children were channelling their headmaster. *"Set the tolerance high. Keep a secret."* The sing-song tone resumed. "Remember, it's *our* secret."

Pierce ran after Claude, trying to make sense of what he had heard.

"Did they talk to you?" asked Claude.

"No," said Pierce. "Nothing happened."

The two men continued in silence. Five minutes later, they turned right at a T-junction and walked along an avenue until they arrived at a church. Claude pointed at a house on the other side of the road.

"That's it, next door but one to the petrol station. It's the bridge of my ship—and the bridge to my world."

"It reminds me of Paxton's past—of the house where his mother lived. I watched him go back there. He was my protégé, and I kept an eye on him. I was afraid he might…"

"Perhaps the ship was expecting you," said Claude. "And this is its way of saying hello, of making you feel at home."

They crossed the empty road—the blacktop decorated with tyre marks and oil stains—and stood on the pavement —with its artificial chewing-gum spots—and regarded the pebble-dashed house. The net curtains moved.

"It's a nosey-neighbour effect—also courtesy of the ship."

"Brilliant, Claude, quite brilliant. What a ship! You're a genius."

Claude's mouth twitched into a half smile. "Thanks." He pushed open the rickety gate—creosoted but unoiled—and walked up the short path. He held out a key. "The lock's my idea, I do have *some* input."

Pierce wondered why a ship that could build a town would leave locks off the doors. It's humouring Claude, he thought. It's giving him something to do. It's therapy, and it's letting me know—winking at me through the interface.

They stepped inside.

"Where's the portal?" Pierce looked around, half expecting to find a glistening curtain hanging across the hallway.

"It's down in the cellar. Come on."

Claude opened the door under the stairs, reached inside, and flipped a switch. Pale yellow light showed bricks with ageing whitewash. A coil of wire hung on a nail, and a hacksaw hung on a hook. A small shelf held dry tins and ancient bottles. The cellar smelt old, and damp, and unvisited.

They climbed down into cool air, and Claude stopped at the foot of the stairs. "This," he said, pointing to a small annexe immediately in front of him, "is it."

Pierce squinted at the jumble of boxes. Offcuts of wood leant against the left-hand wall, and a model ship lay broken on the floor. Books mouldered in a stack, and everything was covered in coal dust. "It's not very grand for a time gateway."

Motes sparkled across the entrance, as if someone had shaken glitter from the ceiling.

"It's open," said Claude. "Go through."

And they stepped into another world.

Claude's House

They arrived in the narrow passageway of a small terraced house. Claude walked through the front door, and onto the porch.

Pierce followed and looked up, squinting at the milky sky. The air outside was cool, but the street was bright and cheery, with bunting looped between the houses. And trestle tables—covered in white cloth, and laden with pies, and cakes, and urns of tea—stood in the road.

When Pierce had crossed the portal—and felt the fizz of the spanning—he had expected to find a shining city in the clouds. Or a wide desert-boulevard lined with fat-bottomed palms, and busy with street vendors and hover cars. Or maybe an undersea dome with luminous creatures crawling over it. Or even the deck of a great spaceship with sweeping views of the galaxy. Things he had dreamed of— tantalising visions—anything but this.

"You look disappointed," said Claude.

"It's not what I expected. I thought your world would be more *dramatic*."

"It's not my world—it's my house. We're standing in my dining room."

"It's a street from the end of World War Two," said Pierce.

"No, it just *looks* that way. It's an interface that *simulates* a street."

"It's very convincing," said Pierce as he stared at a house with a blue door and what looked like an attached workroom.

"I chose 1945," said Claude, "because war had finished, and things were in perspective. Technology had not taken over—and I find that comforting. Everything was more deeply real."

Pierce nodded. "Ironic then that it's a simulation. Still, I have to say that your dining room—with its VE Day auto-buffet—is magnificent." He reached for a cake, "May I? I missed dessert."

"Of course. It's real food—always fresh and always there. Grab a couple of teas while you're at it."

"If this is your dining room," said Pierce, "then where's your front door?"

Claude pointed to a side street. "Two blocks that way."

They walked, munching and slurping, along what looked like a backstreet but was actually Claude's hallway.

"It's built by the ship," said Claude.

"I'm sorry?"

"The interior of my home," said Claude, and he swept his arm in a wide arc, taking in the road, the houses, and the sky, "is powered by the ship's interface engines. The result's not as good as the world *inside* the ship, but it's not bad."

"I assumed it was made by engines in your world, not your ship."

"Our technology's good, but it's not that good. It's all done by the ship—it's a very powerful machine."

"Then—?" Pierce stopped himself.

"Then what?" asked Claude.

Pierce fumbled for another question. "And if the engines stop?"

"My house gets small and boring." Claude sped up. "We're on what amounts to an immersive treadmill. Keeps me fit."

Pierce remembered his far more modest ship, whose interface engines had struggled to create a Victorian office. It lacked the power to decorate its own hallways, let alone bits of the world outside. But Claude's time ship had built towns. Inside *and* out. And yet its technology was beyond Claude's time...

Claude stopped and indicated the crossroads. "This kerb marks the position of my front door. Walk into the road and you'll be out of my house and in my city."

Claude's World

They stepped into the deserted junction, and the blacktop beneath their feet became a tiled patio. The houses opposite, and the narrow roads and footpaths, vanished. The backstreet along which they had walked—Claude's cleverly decorated passage—was now walled off by golden stone, and a door—two humans high—latched closed, where once the kerbstone stood.

A flight of steps led down to a wide and sunny boulevard. Fat-bottomed palm trees—the ones that Pierce had expected—lined the busy street.

"What sort of place is this?" asked Pierce, staring at the crowds below. "It looks like ancient Rome or the Riviera."

"It's a mishmash of antique styles, and everyone's good-looking. It's like an exuberant California. Come on." And he walked down slate steps and into his sparkling city.

"No vehicles," observed Pierce.

"Not here, but there are boats in the canals—there's something of Venice here, too. I'll take you there."

"I like it," said Pierce. He glanced down at his own drab suit. "Once I change my clothes, I'll fit in nicely."

A man approached them in the market square. He looked about sixty, and he wore a loose yellow robe and a silver medallion. He put a hand on Claude's shoulder. "Solved it yet?"

"Working on it, Lex, working on it. Allow me to introduce my friend and collaborator, Pierce Temple." He turned to Pierce. "Pierce, this is Lex Ovidus, my overseer for over a hundred years. A great orator and lawyer."

Pierce extended his hand. "Delighted to meet you."

Lex nodded. "Delighted to meet *you*, Pierce." He gave a slight bow and walked away. "I'm still waiting, Claude."

Claude ignored Lex's standard farewell and smiled at Pierce. "Lost for words?"

"Mmm, sort of."

"Lex is a supercilious old bastard, but at three hundred years old—and as leader of the senate—he has to cultivate a certain disdain. And he *has* been waiting a while…"

"What's he waiting for?"

"Answers."

"So am I." Pierce grinned.

"In that case, let's have lunch by the canal, and I'll fill you in."

"I should be full," said Pierce, jumping on the double meaning—thinking of everything that his mind had just absorbed, and wondering at his rumbling belly. "But I'm not."

"Time travel and world hopping play havoc with your guts. They certainly make me overeat—then I have to exercise."

"Hence your treadmill house." Pierce grinned. "With its street-long rooms."

"Exactly, my house *and* my ship have greatly extended interfaces. That way I have to walk everywhere—and often uphill. Sometimes it's uphill there *and* back. It's all very clever—and designed to trick the mind."

"Your house has a running buffet and a walking street..."

"Yes, it gives *and* takes. But things are far worse *inside* the ship, believe me. Everything's scaled up. If the ship thinks that I've overindulged—which I tend to do on my travels—then it steepens the slopes in the park, it tilts the paths in the town, adds a few more roads, lengthens the avenues, and drives sleeting rain in my face."

"But you have your little car..."

"It won't start—not if the ship's annoyed with my diet. Now, let's go to my favourite restaurant. We can sit outside and admire the view."

The table was covered by a crisp white cloth, the champagne flutes were full, and the first course arrived with a flourish and a smile. The waiter stood back, admiring the dishes. "Enjoy."

"We will," said Claude, resting his elbow on the railing. "It's my favourite."

Pierce poked the giant prawns. "I'm vegetarian."

"They *are* vegetables—farming technology has moved on since your time. Now, eat up and enjoy the fruits—literally the fruits—of this advanced civilisation that has taken you in—albeit unwittingly—as a refugee."

"We had false meat, too, you know," said Pierce. He crunched through prawn husk, wiped his mouth, and grinned. "But this is superb. I suppose you'll have steak for the main course?"

"Mammoth is on special. But I prefer tandoori dodo…"

Pierce stared at the canal. "How far back have you gone?"

"Dinosaur tastes like chicken." Claude smirked. "Just joking. Everything these days is vegetarian—or at least cultured without sentience. Everything moves on. Even morality. Many people object to artificial animal meat. Porno-food, they call it." He crunched into a fat veggie-prawn. "They consider it bad taste. They think that vegetables should *look* like vegetables."

"Purists," said Pierce, "are always a problem."

A gondola slipped by with a courting couple—both female—holding hands. The gondolier waved at Claude. "Another busy day, Señor Claudius?"

"I'm afraid so, Fred—one of the busiest ever, actually. But you're taking it easy, I see."

"My life is the canal, Señor—and the canal is always easy. Take care."

"Fred? Señor? Not exactly Venetian, is it?" Pierce stared at the receding boat.

"We pick and choose and mix things up. We're not slavish copiers, you know. This quarter is Venice *reimagined*."

"Can you really improve on the original?" asked Pierce.

"You'd be surprised. For one thing, it's not sinking."

"Surely that was part of its charm: the sense of impermanence, and the encroaching sea."

"Only for tourists. Imagine building a collapsing city. Imagine the legal implications. Imagine what Lex would say. Still, we do our best, and the place *looks* like it's sinking. It's a compromise. And a great challenge to the architects. And a source of constant debate."

"It works," said Pierce, glancing at a tilting arcade. "It really does."

Claude nodded. "Some people pump water into their cellars, but I think that's going too far."

"An underground pool sounds nice—and very convenient."

"I suppose so," said Claude, rubbing his belly. "But the thought of water beneath my sitting room would unsettle me. And things are unsettled enough as it is."

"I really like it here," said Pierce. "In fact, I might love it."

"After lunch, we'll visit the art gallery. Then you'll be hooked."

"No rush," said Pierce. "I'm looking forward to pudding, and more champagne."

They staggered along a narrow path, over a narrow bridge, under a covered bridge, along another narrow path, past a hat shop nestled in an archway, over another bridge, and then Claude stopped at the corner of a leaning palace.

Pierce rocked unsteadily. "This it?"

"Mmm." Claude leant against a wooden door, and they half fell into a dingy corridor. "The gallery's upstairs, come on."

The exhibition space had exposed beams on its walls and ceiling, and the floorboards were buffed by age. Strange antique piping edged the skirting boards, clicking and burbling away like the heating tubes in an old schoolroom.

"The floor's tilted!" exclaimed Pierce, holding out his arms to balance.

"No, it's not. And it's not the champagne. It's the cunning architecture—the clever angles, tapering boards, and misaligned windows." He tapped his toe on a floorboard. "See that glass tube set in the wood?"

Pierce nodded.

"It's a spirit level," said Claude.

Pierce bent down and ran his finger along the glass. "I've found the bubble."

"And where is it?"

"Immediately under the centreline." Pierce stood up and scanned the floor. "In fact, there are strips of glass everywhere. Half the boards have tubes."

"The architects were proud of their illusion, so they put spirit levels all over the place. And that's a plumb line, next to the only vertical window."

"You can't argue with physics," said Pierce, squinting at a teardrop of lead hanging from a golden thread. "But the false perspective makes me seasick."

"The designers wanted you to notice their gallery before you noticed the art. They were jealous, and they strayed from their brief. But it's impossible to prove, since the whole building was meant to look like it was subsiding. Lex tried suing, but he failed, and now he refuses to come here. He still bitches about it, and he takes it out on me. But now you know, so you can ignore the twisted room and enjoy the pictures." He grinned. "Beautiful, aren't they?"

The paintings—hanging on grey plaster walls—were lit by invisible spotlights, making them glow like screens.

"Are the lights too bright?" asked Pierce, trying to focus on a rosy nude and hovering cherubs. "The colours are very intense."

"It's the Renaissance as she really was," said Claude.

Pierce ignored him and stared at the far wall, where a painting of a woman had captured his attention. "I *must* see this," he said, and wobbled over to inspect the portrait.

They stood before the picture, with their hands lightly clasped behind their backs, trying their best to look like critics. The painted woman stared back with the hint of a smile. Her hands were lightly clasped in front, and she seemed to be mocking them.

"It's a perfect copy," said Claude.

Pierce shook his head. "No, the colours are too bright. No one would mistake it for the *real* Mona Lisa."

"It's very new," said Claude.

Pierce squinted. "Who painted it?"

"Leonardo—or at least a perfect copy of him."

Pierce blinked. "I need another drink."

"Me too," said Claude. "Let's go."

Drinks

They walked by the canal and watched the late afternoon bustle.

"I know just the spot," said Claude, and he led Pierce over a bridge, down a narrow alley, and past a tiny shop.

Pierce stopped. "That's interesting." He peered at the model ships in the window. "It's the *Great Eastern*," he said, pointing at a steamship about a metre long. "Aart, my main protégé, was very fond of that ship. He had a picture of it in his study. The model's beautifully done."

"It's made entirely of glass—rigging, sails, smoke, the lot. Come on, let's have that drink."

The place that Claude chose was dark and cramped, with low ceilings, and exposed beams, and leaded windows. And deep inside it glowed, like a country pub.

"I don't know what it is," said Pierce, leaning on the bar and looking at the shelves of whiskey, "but all I want is champagne. I used to like red wine, and the occasional malt."

"The spanning locked the taste of champagne in your head."

Pierce frowned.

"You'd finished a whole bottle when I rescued you." Claude raised a hand as Pierce started to object. "Perfectly understandable—it *was* the end of your world. Then you got into my ship, and time travel churns the psyche—and things take root in loosened minds. If you'd been listening to music, you'd have a tune stuck in your head."

"Like in adolescence, when memories impress themselves in the re-wiring brain?"

"Exactly," said Claude. "And it makes you wonder what all this time travelling does to our minds. In the long term, I mean."

"Keeps us young, I suppose."

"We get moments of youthfulness, but the effect fades," said Claude. "Spanning brings clarity, but it doesn't last— it's just a brief lucidity, at an unknown cost."

The barman arrived. "Yes, sir?"

Claude leant across and whispered his order. He turned back to Pierce. "Let's sit by the window."

A waiter arrived with a golden bottle in an ice bucket of blue glass. "Enjoy, gentlemen."

"We will," said Claude, "my friend here is something of an enthusiast."

"Indeed, sir." The waiter retreated, leaving the two men to themselves.

"Well?" said Pierce. "You promised answers—answers that Lex is yet to receive."

"Lex—genius that he is—is not ready for the answers that I have."

"But you think that I am?" asked Pierce with a smile.

"Yes," said Claude, "not because you're smarter than he is—no one is, although his talents lie more in politics and law—but because you've jumped from a dying world. And he has not."

Bubble's End

"Not again." Pierce stared out, barely registering the passersby who rippled beyond the faux Elizabethan glass. His eyes brimmed with tears and his right hand twitched. His champagne stood untouched. "Another world ends."

"I'm sorry, Pierce, I really am. But it's better that you know."

"This is how Aart must have felt." Pierce watched a group of clowns walk past. "Aart had no hope of rescue. In fact, he had no hope. And he killed himself. But I was rescued once…"

"We won't be saved. There's no mentor here. Lex is my only senior—and he's no scientist."

"No one left you notes?"

"No…" Claude looked out, his gaze parallel to Pierce's. Now a group of girls trooped past. They wore papier-mâché masks with hooked beaks and devil tongues and vampire teeth. And their perfect figures were hugged by motley cloth. They giggled and span and jigged along—a blur of red and black and gold.

"You had no mentor, yet you made a time ship. You created bubbles without help." Pierce swigged his drink.

"Yes." Claude poured more champagne, and they drank in silence.

"But your...?"

Claude raised his eyebrows. "My what?"

"Nothing," said Pierce. "It doesn't matter."

"God help us," said Pierce, playing along. "If we're not in a bubble, then this is the final fire. *This is it.*"

"It's worse than that. We won't just run out of time—like bubble dwellers—we'll run out of everything. We're under attack, and reality—even the past—is collapsing. And it's my fault!" Claude drained his champagne.

"Can't we make bubbles to hide in? You know, *keep going back?*"

"Maybe, for the short-term, but history's collapsing. Running to a bubble would be like climbing on a table in a sinking ship."

Pierce sniffed. "But..."

"There's nowhere to run." Claude sighed and stood up. "There really isn't. Let's go back to the ship, and I'll show you." He went over to the bar and paid—in a way that Pierce did not understand—and they stumbled out.

Weatherman

Partygoers surged in the streets, and Pierce and Claude fought the human tide. Masks and daubed faces — pretty and vacant and nodding — loomed and vanished. The pseudo-antique walls rang with the music of trumpets and bells and tambourines.

"Divine joke," said Pierce.

"What?"

"Carnival and carnage, the gods — "

A girl harlequin slammed into Pierce, squealed, grabbed his cheeks, kissed him hard on the lips, shuddered, curtsied, and ran on.

Claude grinned. "There are consolations, even now."

"Especially now — the gods taunt, and give us sport in the final moments."

They stood by the high door in the pale golden wall. Below, the twilit boulevard swarmed. Lanterns hung from palms. Strings of lights crisscrossed the street. A rapt group watched a man swallow a sword. And a ballerina — surreal even here — sobbed on a kerb.

The door swung open—without a key or handle—and they stepped into silence and into the street that was Claude's long hallway. He walked in front: first hunched, then upright, twitching and shaking, desolate, and distracted, and determined. The empty windows looked on, keeping their counsel.

The trestle tables creaked under the weight of cakes and ale.

Pierce licked his lips. "Mind if I have a beer?"

"Help yourself. And grab some orange sponge as well. The house is doing its best, so you might as well take advantage." Claude smiled. "It sounds like your champagne fixation is weakening…"

Pierce bit his cake and felt its tang. He sipped his beer and stared at the bunting—bright against grey clouds—and thought of Acantha's urging to watch the sky. But this was no sky, just a painted ceiling in Claude's house. And that said it all.

"Let's go," said Claude. "I have a simulator in my ship. It'll explain everything."

Pierce followed—dribbling beer and dropping crumbs, like a Hansel in the woods—through the narrow doorway in the narrow house, and through the shimmering portal, and back to Claude's time ship.

They emerged at the foot of the cellar steps. The pale yellow bulb still shone, and coal dust still hung in the air. The last confetti-like sparkles vanished as the portal closed, and Pierce smiled at the cleverness of the interface. "OK, where's your simulator?"

"Upstairs, disguised as a television."

They climbed into warm household air and headed for the lounge room. There was a settee, and two armchairs, and a coffee table loaded with papers and magazines. Dust motes floated in beams of sunlight, and a cup of tea sat half-drunk next to a plate of biscuits. A primitive colour TV stood in the corner. It had a plastic-wood cabinet, a bulbous curving screen, and dark slots for the sound. The two chairs held the impressions of recently vanished backsides.

Pierce grinned. "So this is the bridge of your ship—it's a proper *Mary Celeste*."

"Glad you noticed. My ship loves its conceits. Now watch this."

Claude walked over to the TV. A crackle and a flash, the snowy picture resolved, and a tinny voice came out.

"It's the weather…" said Pierce.

The TV presenter frowned—as if annoyed by the interruption—and banged his chart.

"Strange map," said Pierce. "Where is it?"

"Everywhere—those shapes aren't coastlines, they're universes. And the arrows are the voyages of time travellers. That big red arrow is me, and the thin blue one is you."

"Turn it up," said Pierce. "I don't want to miss anything."

Claude obliged. "Don't worry. He loops and updates, and the forecast is always the same…"

"What we have here," said the weatherman, tapping the arrows that curved across his chart, "is a series of visits to the past." He indicated the vertical tube shape. "This column is the real world—the actual *trunk of history*." He turned to face Claude.

Claude shifted uncomfortably. "The ship made him, but he still unsettles me…"

The weatherman pursed his lips and glared. He pivoted and stared at his peculiar map. "As you can see, the arrows touch the trunk and cause buds to balloon out." He ran his finger around a circle—containing its own fine lines and thin arrows—that was attached to the stem by a narrow isthmus. "This is a bubble-world." He turned to Claude. "This red arrow—the one piercing the circle—is Claude visiting a bubble world—a little universe that he made himself."

"Copied, rather than made," corrected Claude. "It's a glitch…"

The weatherman coughed impatiently.

"That's *my* world…" said Pierce. He reached back to grab the arms of the nearer chair, and lowered himself into the waiting cushion. "That circle is my *whole* world." The arrows and circles in the TV chart reminded him of the playground's chalky design. Keep quiet, he told himself, that was a private message.

"And here," announced the weatherman, pointing at the root of the bubble world, "is the problem."

Tiny circles streamed from the isthmus and from its origin in the main trunk. In a primitive and jerky animation, they split and coalesced and drifted across the chart. And, for a moment, it looked like symbolic weather spreading across a real television map. And the ship-generated avatar looked like a real weatherman standing in a distant studio. And it sounded as if he were describing a moving storm, and his words—occasionally masked by static—seem to arrive on old-fashioned radio waves. Then the moment passed.

Pierce's jaw fell slack. Claude shuffled. And outside, a bird—also ship-generated—sang. Not a nightingale's call or a parrot's squawk, but a high lament.

The weatherman grew, and his eyes burned. "Copying has consequences!" he screamed, his face filling the screen. "It always does!"

Claude's fingers trembled. He licked his lips, and—like Pierce had done moments earlier—he backed into a chair and slumped into its already concave cushion.

The TV picture cut to a close-up of the tiny circles that foamed around the branch point on the trunk of history. The weatherman's voice rang from every corner of the room as the ship dispensed with its avatar and spoke directly to the two men on the bridge. "These membranous fragments were released like sawdust when the bubble world was formed. They drifted across that non-place that lies outside the trunk of history—and they took on a life of their own. They merged and exchanged material—a sort of bubble sex —and then they split like bacteria. They invaded the trunk —like fungus invades an oak—and rotted history."

Claude jumped from his chair. "It's mixing similes," he wept. "I'll have to adjust it."

The television cracked. The ship screamed, "No!" And the screen went black.

Coming to Terms

They stood in the front garden. Claude leant on the rickety gate, stared at the church opposite, and shook his head. "The ship's not happy, it broke through its interface. It left the television and stepped out of character."

Pierce looked down the street to the distant tower of another church. "Maybe the weatherman's wrong, maybe the ship's lying..."

"I doubt it. Copying a section of history could create friction, and particles could escape into the void and corrode the trunk. It's plausible."

"How can you build a time machine and not know these things?" asked Pierce. "You must have considered the consequences. You must have wrestled with paradoxes."

"It was easy..."

"But you had no mentor, no one was guiding you..."

Claude shook his head. "I had a head start."

"How do you mean?" Pierce leant forward.

"There was a kind of egg," said Claude.

"An egg?"

Claude nodded. "It just arrived—a foundling in my room."

"Then what happened?" asked Pierce. "Did it hatch?"

"No, nothing like that. It flew at a wall and well, it..."

"It what?" prompted Pierce.

"It burrowed into the stone and made a portal, and I, er, I stepped through it. After that, I pretty much knew what to do."

"How? Were there instructions? Was someone there to help?"

"No," said Claude. "I just knew—intuitively. And I read stuff in a book."

"A book?"

"Yes, a science fiction story—it was just lying around, and I got ideas from it."

"We think we're geniuses," said Pierce. He looked across at an arched window, and he found himself counting courses, in an echo of Paxton's counting. And for much the same reason: to prove—by examining details—that this place was real. "We think we're gods."

"Lex doesn't think I'm a god. Lex is pissed off."

"Why?"

"Certain *irregularities*—mainly to do with paintings and their provenance. In short, he thinks I'm a criminal— that I'm hiding forgers in cellars. But all I've done is brought genuine copies of great art to enrich this place—to decorate this *New Venice* of his."

"Lex has no idea about your time machine?"

"None whatsoever—even less that by meddling in time I'm demolishing history." Claude squirmed. "I'm good at keeping secrets, big ones, anyway."

"You should talk to him," said Pierce. "Try to put his mind at ease."

"You're right. I can't deal with his harping—not when I'm facing the end of history. It's too much. *I have to concentrate*. I can't have him witter. He just won't leave me alone..."

Quintina Mariana Thrash

Lex stared Claude straight in the eye. "That's complete bollocks!"

Claude turned to Pierce and shrugged. "I tried."

"You're lying," said Lex. "You're up to no good with your paintings, but don't go overboard with stories of time machines. In any case, pictures—forged or otherwise—aren't the pressing issue."

"They're not?" said Claude, brightening. "Are you having more trouble with the architects? I've heard rumblings about the sculpture room..."

"No, it's *your* activities—your *manufacturing* activities. You're polluting this beautiful place."

Claude frowned. "I am?"

"Don't come the innocent with me. I spoke to experts. The climate's changing, and the weather's all wrong."

"How do you mean?" asked Claude. He shuffled uncomfortably, thinking of all the factories that had licenced his technologies—and made him rich.

Lex raised his right arm, as if he were about to spout rhetoric. "Just look at the sky!"

The clouds were thick and creamy, like plastic, and the blue had drained away.

Pierce smiled as he realised that this world—and all its temporal corrosion, so graphically shown by the weatherman—was a mere bubble. And that implied a creator—a time traveller who had made this bubble and who should, if Pierce and Claude were anything to go by, feel compassion for his protégés. "I hope your benefactor has set the tolerance of his ship, to what?"

"Oh, at least five hundred percent," said Claude, picking up on Pierce's relief at the changing sky. "That way, we can take Lex with us. We could do with a good lawyer in the next level. And then he can aggravate them instead of me..."

"What the hell are you two blathering about?"

But Claude had stopped listening. He stared over Lex's shoulder and pointed. The ancient politician—and the best legal mind in the world—span round.

A shimmering portal had opened, and a woman who looked in her early thirties climbed out. Her features were fine and highly evolved, and her eyes were large and liquid and green. She smiled. "I'm Quintina Mariana Thrash. Please come aboard. And hurry—we don't have much time."

PART THREE

QUINTINA

Black Roof

They followed the woman through her gateway and into a world of shadow and sunlight, arches and warm stone. A square of lawn lay outside, beyond the arcade. Leaded windows set in high walls looked onto the grass where tiny birds—bright but unknown—picked for food. There was murmuring, like distant conversation, but they were quite alone.

Pierce grabbed his belly and squinted—giddy from the spanning—trying to make sense of the new place, and feeling the hunger. "Are we in Oxford?"

"It's a quad," announced Quintina, marching down the cloister, waving at the carved faces in the walls. "The heads are modelled on philosophers. It's based on several universities, and a couple of monasteries. I gave the ship a free hand." She turned to face the men and smiled, proud of an interface that wasn't hers. "It's a place of contemplation. A place that keeps the world at bay. It calms me. And it has many doors, so it's quite convenient."

"What's happened?" asked Lex. "Where are we?"

"We're in my ship," said Quintina. "Claude and Pierce can explain."

Lex grunted and reached for a pillar. "Claude has a lot of explaining to do." But Lex was soothed by the architecture, and took comfort in its details. After the jump, he needed to stop and take stock—like a rushed traveller, arriving in a new city, might pause to contemplate the ornamental brickwork of the railway station.

"I don't see many doors," said Pierce.

"They're hidden in plain sight," said Quintina. "So, the temptation to walk across the grass should be resisted."

Pierce nodded. "The arches…"

Quintina stopped. "Yes, every archway is a portal. The lawn out there is quite unreachable—it's pure illusion. We're standing in a beautiful interchange."

"So if I step through," said Pierce. And he vanished.

A moment later he was back, ashen and shaking.

"Well?" asked Quintina. "Where did you go?"

"I think I was on the Eiffel Tower, at night in an old Paris. You know, when the tower still stood. When Paris was…"

"My favourite place," said Quintina, gazing into a treasured past. "Or it was, before the war." She rallied. "But you have to be prepared before making a jump like that." She looked from one to the other. "I'll take you somewhere lower, since Pierce, judging from his face, hates heights." She walked along the flagstones and stopped by a narrow corner arch. "This will do." She stepped through and vanished.

Pierce and Claude followed, popping into nothingness, framed as they went by the faintest of sparkles.

Lex stood in the cloistered quad of time doors and shivered. Wind rushed down the passage, making the carved heads chatter and complain like old men in winter. The chatter became a scream, and Lex ran.

They were in another walkway. But this was a tunnel, whose curved walls were dull and damp and green, and a far cry from the airy cloister of a moment ago.

"Follow me," said Quintina. "You'll like this place."

They walked into a wide chamber and waited for their eyes to adjust to the gloom. Lex and Claude and Pierce stared at the black ceiling. Luminous squiggles and occasional flashes broke the darkness.

"It looks," said Pierce, "like a hectic planetarium."

"It's an undersea observatory," said Quintina. "And the stars you saw were fish—mostly."

"And the others?" asked Pierce, thrilled by the thin blade of déjà vu.

"They're a mix of mutant molluscs and bioluminescent microbes. The dome attracts things from miles around, *and they try to get in.*"

"I hope the glass holds," said Lex, still trembling.

"There's no glass," said Quintina, "just a force field—then kilometres of seawater. The field's hum draws the creatures in. They find it irresistible, and so the ocean beyond is quite depleted."

Lex's eyes widened, and his right hand twitched. "We're privileged, then." He tracked a glowing eel as it squirmed above. And a skull-thing, with a spray of needle-teeth, hammered silently on the dome. Something milky heaved and fluttered at the perimeter, and a meteor-shower of bright green dots arced across the roof.

"Why are we here?" asked Pierce.

"Aesthetics."

"And?" prompted Pierce, knowing that Quintina was toying with him.

"To give you confidence in your visions."

"What's that mean, Pierce?" asked Lex, squinting at what looked like a zombie fish covered in fairy lights. The fish regarded Lex with dark intelligence, shook its head, and swam off to peer at a throbbing sac that inched across the seafloor. Lex rotated to watch.

"I expected this place," said Pierce. He looked at Quintina. "That's what you meant, wasn't it?"

"Yes. Your precognition is a talent I'll use. A talent which—in the original trunk—*you* used." She pursed her lips and stared into nothing. "Of course that happened later —and to a different you."

A twist of lights, and the zombie fish gobbled up the sac. It eyed Lex through a cloud of spawn, waiting for his reaction.

"Pierce sees the future," said Lex, glaring at the fish. "And we're in an underwater horror show." The fish turned, flicked its tail, and sailed off.

"It's an underwater *observatory*," said Quintina.

Lex shuffled, rammed his hands into his pockets, and sniffed. He stared at his shoes, annoyed and slighted and peculiarly aroused—first by the fish, and then by the woman.

Pierce wandered up to the invisible wall that held back the sea. An eye—connected to a blurry thing with tentacles —pressed against the dome. Pierce poked it. "Aah!" He stared at his dripping finger.

The leggy thing flapped, squirted, went scarlet, and vanished.

"You scared it," said Quintina, and grinned.

"It scared *me*," said Pierce.

"You could have let it in," said Lex. "It could have exploded—right here on the floor, because of the pressure drop."

"Your discomfiture is amusing," said Quintina, "but the only one at risk was Pierce," she turned to the shaking man who was staring at his wet finger as if its tip had gone, "who did an incredibly stupid thing. If you'd put your head through, and gone eye-to-eye with the squid, then the field would have closed around your neck. The squid's beak would have sliced your face off, and the water pressure would have crushed your skull. Not that you'd have known, it would have been over in less than a second. Then a small feeding frenzy…"

"Bloody dangerous," said Lex, "but amusing—at least for those inside the dome."

"Stupidity," said Quintina, "is why this undersea palace got shut down a hundred years ago. A whole school group lost their heads after a dare. The place was totally abandoned after that, but the field still runs. See that pale ring?"

The three men nodded, observing a grey line that ran around the floor, two metres from the water face.

"That was where the old wall stood—the one the children vaulted over. Sometimes, at night—not that night means much down here—you can hear their laughter turn to screams."

They trooped out. Pierce looked back through the tunnel at the pale ring on the floor, and he pictured ghost children clambering over the vanished wall, and running to the curving sea. And he saw the foremost pushing their heads against the force field, and having their faces ripped off. He heard the screams of those at the back, and the thud of tiny bodies, and the gasps of their teacher. And the screeching alarm.

He grabbed the railings of the school gate, staring at an empty playground full of voices—

"Pierce!"

Quintina's yell dragged him back to the moment. He turned and trudged from the dome, along the dismal passage, and he knew that Quintina's ship had sent him a message—coded, like a dream—via Claude's ship. It was far cleverer than Quintina, for all her bluster. It had spoken to him through the layers, showing him ghost children in a school—and foreshadowing her invented horror story. A story that made no sense. She's lying, he thought, about the children, and everything else.

Black Sky

They returned to the quad—with its imaginary lawn—and Quintina led them along another side of the enclosed garden. She stopped at the large central arch, whose stony sides sparkled.

"We'll go through here. I'm sure you'll appreciate the contrast." She stepped towards the grass and vanished.

Lex and Claude and Pierce followed her through the arch, and the quad's blue sky went black. They found themselves standing on an invisible floor, in the middle of a vast and glassy sphere. Beyond this perfect window—in all directions—lay a glinting night sky.

"They're stars," said Quintina, "real ones."

"Bloody hell," said Pierce, playing his part. "I expected this, too. I see we're in a spaceship."

Quintina smiled as if he were a favoured pupil. She pointed at a triangular table. "Everyone take a seat, and I'll explain why I grabbed you from your bubbles and brought you here."

The three men sat silently through Quintina's prepared speech. When she had finished—which she signalled with a deep sigh—she stepped around the backs of their chairs, and the men swivelled their heads to track her. They frowned and twitched, trying to digest her words. Even Pierce, despite his foresight, was at a loss.

Lex snorted. "Let me get this clear. We investigate crimes. We create tiny bubble worlds that contain the scene of a crime. And then we visit them and watch. In some cases, we do experiments. And we do this again and again until we have analysed the criminal and his—or her—crime to the ultimate degree. Then we present a case—a *watertight* case—to what passes for a court of law in your time."

"Precisely," said Quintina. "Your skill in summing up shines through." She stared at a distant galaxy, no more than a grey smudge in the black nothingness. "You might think that technology would make legal arguments obsolete —that we could present irrefutable evidence and convict every time. And for simple crimes, committed by simple criminals, we can. But we're in an arms race with sophisticated villains—and they have more resources than we have. They can subvert witnesses, twist evidence, and simulate plausible alternatives—so much so that no one knows what's real anymore. And they're winning." She twitched. *"My enemies—"*

"Enemies?" asked Lex.

"Just a figure of speech…" She sniffed and stiffened. "Criminals are *everyone's* enemy."

"Sounds exciting," said Pierce. She needs us, he thought, because we're strangers. We have no history here. We don't know what's happened in this world. And this world doesn't know us. "Count me in."

"Oh, you're all in, believe me."

"You mean we have no choice, Ms Thrash?" asked Lex. *"What if we want to do something else?"*

"You were *created* for this. *I made your bubbles. I made your worlds*. All nested. All my own work. *And I can reverse it*." She stepped back, pausing for emphasis—letting the backdrop of stars add weight to her threat. She thumped the table. "I grab the bubbles from history. And you visit them. *And report back*."

She can't reverse it, thought Pierce. She's bluffing: bubbles can't be undone—they stay in the void. You can't uncopy a bubble.

Lex stared at the woman. "My only hope, Ms Thrash, is that you too have been cultivated by a yet greater personage. And that you too will be called—kicking and screaming—to a higher duty."

"Isn't he perfect?" she said, clapping her hands like a schoolgirl. "Just perfect!" She turned to the old patrician. "Lex, you're a credit to your real-life counterpart—you'll simply *destroy* those defence lawyers."

"When do we begin?" asked Pierce, forcing his face to look open and keen.

"Right away. Your first mystery is the death of the architect of this ship, my old friend Cosmo."

First Case

Lex and Claude and Pierce sat in a windowless room in Quintina's time ship and stared at a file. It was an old-fashioned thing—all papers and photographs spilling from a manilla folder. And it was spread across an old-fashioned desk. And no one really knew what to do about it.

"As you can see," said Quintina, who paced and clattered. "It's a murder."

"It says suicide," observed Pierce, holding a page of type in one hand and a photograph of a grizzled old man in the other. "There's no evidence of foul play."

"Cosmo would never kill himself," said Quintina. "There's more to it than that. He built this time ship. He had everything to live for. He was happy. And stable."

The man in the photo—the dead Cosmo—had a beard and a twinkling eye, and he looked like the perfect captain for a time ship. Despite his jovial expression, he was muscular and alert—a natural commander and engineer—and well able to take care of himself. No one would have sneaked up on Cosmo.

She's lying again. "You're right," said Pierce. "He *does* look happy." *But that means nothing. Someone can look happy one moment and die by their own hand that very day. Who can tell?*

"You have to investigate." She rested her hands on Pierce's shoulders. "I'll send you back well before his death. Feel the atmosphere. Listen to what he says. Keep your eyes open. *Be discreet.*"

Pierce nodded. "OK."

Quintina swept from the room, and Pierce followed— raising his eyebrows and shrugging at the still seated Lex and Claude—playing the anointed pupil to her school mistress.

Lex pushed himself up. "Can't miss this."

"I agree," said Claude.

Quintina led them down a burnished corridor and into another featureless room.

"We leave from here," she announced.

"OK," said Pierce, looking around.

"Tell him you're a friend of mine and he'll talk to you. He looks gruff, but he's friendly. Talk about time machines —he knows I understand them, so you'll sound genuine. And he loves boasting about his ship. But don't even hint that you're from the future."

"I'm from the past…"

"You're *leaving* from the future."

"Fair enough."

"Remember, he's very smart. Don't try to be clever. And observe. *Details*, Pierce, *details*."

"OK." He looked down. "What about my clothes? Surely, fashions are different..."

"Anything goes in this world. Some idiots dress as knights, and some as cavemen. Believe me, you'll fit in. In any case, you'll only see Cosmo, and, like most engineers, he barely notices what people wear."

"Speech?"

"Don't try to be difficult, Pierce. You have an educated, albeit slightly archaic, manner and a neutral accent—neutral by this world's standards, anyway. You'll be fine." She sniffed. "Ready now?"

Pierce nodded.

Quintina tapped the curved wall—hitting a button that only she could see—and then her fingers danced across the metal as if she were playing a piano. A portal opened with a click. "We're through."

Still using her left hand, she drew an invisible design next to the shimmering gateway, her forefinger looping and swiping. Her lips were pursed, and her head was tilted. She frowned, like a child absorbed in her art, then she stepped back, as if admiring the result. Another tap on the unseen button. "The tolerance is set at five percent, so don't bring anything back. And watch for signs. *Observe everything*."

And Pierce was doing just that: tracking her movements, memorising the code.

"The portal opens in a cupboard," she continued. "Listen before opening the door. When you climb out, turn right. The corridor is open—rather like my cloister—and you'll see an ocean on your left. Walk to the door at the end of the passage. Knock and remember to say you're a friend of mine. I have few friends, so he'll be intrigued. And he gets no visitors, not there. The place is very secure, so if you've managed to get in, he'll assume you've been vetted. He's a king in his tower, so treat him as such."

"Sounds straightforward," said Pierce. "Can anything go wrong?"

"Things can always go wrong. If they do, don't try to fix them. Run back to the portal. No one can follow you through. Everything in that world is quarantined from us— it's just a bubble, and it's short-lived. And we can always try again. *So be quick.* Are you ready?"

"Yes," said Pierce, and he stepped through the gateway and felt the tingle of the spanning.

The place was dark—with a smell of wood and paint—and gritty underfoot. There was a crack of light inches from his face. He put his ear to the gap, and some faraway noises filtered through, but no footsteps. And there was the smell of the sea. He slowly breathed to calm his heart.

And he wondered—standing there in his cupboard— why Quintina had sent him here, when she could have gone herself. And then he knew—for the spanning had made his mind race—that she was terrified that someone would stop her from returning to the ship. *But who? Not Lex or Claude or I, for a start we don't know the code.* He pictured her tapping the wall, but the memory of her movements had faded. *She's scared of someone else.*

He poked his head out. There was a stony corridor with a brilliant blue sea beyond its arches. The sky blazed, utterly cloudless. He stepped out and carefully closed the cupboard doors. But they clicked shut—as if grabbed by magnets—and the sound rang out. Pierce walked towards Cosmo's door and, as he tapped along the flagstones, he wondered if the design that Quintina had traced by the portal's edge had really set the tolerance so low…

Cosmo

Cosmo Portus sat at his desk, his fingers steepled, his brow creased, and his right foot tapping on the pale green tiles. Cool air blew across the room and took the edge off the baking day. Beyond his open window, stretched the great harbour. And in the sparkling sea, was a great variety of ships.

"That's the *Great Western*, isn't it?" Pierce pointed at a dark steamship anchored near the jetty. "And over there, I'm sure that's the *Bounty*. And there's the *Victory*. You've got everything here, Cosmo. Even longships."

"No Vikings, though... The ships are all manned by volunteers—historical enthusiasts, of which we have many. But no one wants to be a Viking."

"You couldn't bring them back, then, the original crews?"

"Good heavens, no—and the ships are all replicas. But we got highly detailed scans of them—and fine-grained data on the crews. The model of Nelson—which talks, incidentally—won an award. We built him to stop all the arguments, since so many players fancied themselves in the role."

"How did you cover it up? How did you do all this without revealing your time ship?"

Cosmo cleared his throat. "I said I had a reconstructor —a device that extrapolated from fragments—a machine that cross-checked records and artefacts. I said that it was the most powerful computer ever built. I said that I fed it with historical facts. It was a bit of a white lie, really, but everyone believed me. The historians—who are very powerful in this city—got what they wanted, so no one probed. Gift horses, and all that." Cosmo stared at his marine museum. "I'm glad that Quintina asked you to come. It's been nice chatting to someone who understands. She's very interested in my time machine, you know. But I can't let her near it. God knows what she'd do..."

"She did..."

"Did what?"

"She took your machine." Pierce thrilled as he crossed the line. "She sent me back to check on you."

"Back? Then I'm..." Cosmo prodded his gut and frowned. "Can't be. I'm the same. *Nothing's changed.*" He stared at Pierce. *"Nothing's happened! You're lying! I can remember everything—for years. There was no jump, no glitch. No, it's not possible."*

Pierce shrugged. "You *are* a copy. Copies think they're real, and in all important respects, they *are* real. I'm a copy, and I'm real. There's no difference. A bubble-you is still a you—whatever the word *you* really means…"

Plasticky clouds gathered over the harbour, and the ships bobbed in the roughening sea whose blue had drained to grey. A horn blew, and the hot wind cooled. *Watch for signs.*

"I must go," said Pierce.

Cosmo stood up, and his hands shook. "Can I come?"

Pierce felt his heart break. *Could I take him? Was the tolerance really only five percent? Was Quintina waiting by the portal, drumming her fingers? What happens if you exceed the baggage allowance on a time ship—does everything explode?*

"Quintina set the tolerance at five percent. She was quite definite about that…"

"Bitch…" His lip quivered. He blinked, like an oncologist—who has spent years giving out bad news—finally facing his own test results.

"I'm sorry. I'll try adjusting the ship—"

"Next time," interrupted Cosmo. "For the next version of me…" He spread his hands and stared across his soon-to-vanish harbour, like an admiral facing an unstoppable fleet.

He *was* strong, thought Pierce, just like his photo. Not the sort of man to kill himself.

"I'm sorry, I really am."

Cosmo ignored him.

Pierce slipped from the room, and guilt raked his spine, dragging its broken nails down his skin, making his guts roil and his arms tingle. He ran to the cupboard and flung open its doors. And a sense memory flashed up of an Advent calendar from long ago. He was a child again, and it was nearly Christmas. He was opening a cardboard flap in a dark and snowy forest, breaking through the printed winter to the magic underneath—and feeling the tingle.

He paused and looked back.

Cosmo was staring out to sea, framed by the case of his rarely opened door. But he was hunched now, and he moaned—keening for himself and his dying world.

Pierce stepped onto the cupboard's narrow gritty floor. He stared at the back wall and watched it ripple, then he squared his shoulders, took a deep breath, and walked through the portal—and back into the time ship.

They were all waiting for him. Claude was pacing, like an expectant father. Lex was sniffing. Quintina was upright, her head flung back.

The portal closed with a click, leaving no trace in the wall.

"Well?" asked Claude, wringing his hands. "What happened? Tell us everything!"

"I had a brief chat to Cosmo. He looked fine. Although," Pierce looked at Quintina, "I thought for a moment that he suspected he was in a bubble…"

"Quite possible," said Quintina. "He was a smart man. Never mind. That world's closed, and we can forget about him. I'll send you back closer to the crime time." She stepped to the wall, finger at the ready.

"I need a rest," said Pierce, rubbing his forehead. "And I'm hungry."

"Tomorrow, then," said Quintina, and swept away, "nice and early. I'm going into town. I can point out some good restaurants, if anyone's interested."

Lex followed her out.

"Going for a meal?" asked Pierce, looking at Claude.

Claude shook his head. "You go. And have a champagne for me. I want to explore the ship—it's calling me."

"Don't get lost," said Pierce, but Claude had gone. Sirens should make you leave ships, thought Pierce, not board them. "Be safe, Claude," he whispered, "it's not your ship."

Quintina clicked down the passage. A distant laugh and muffled conversation, then silence. Pierce waited some more. Then he tapped the bronzy wall, and the portal opened with a hiss. He traced a pentagram. "Five hundred percent," he whispered, and as he spoke he knew that his tapping and tracing and speaking were pointless. There was no code. No human could set a time ship.

He stepped through the portal and his mind sharpened. Quintina believes in her codes, he thought. The ship has tricked her. It's Cosmo's ship—and ships, like dogs, have one master.

Portus

Pierce stood in Cosmo's office. "I know Quintina."

It was nine o'clock, and already hot. The wind blew across the tiles, the boats bobbed in the harbour, blue birds twittered on the veranda, and Cosmo looked up from his desk. "Delighted to meet you. You're a friend?"

"No," said Pierce, "a colleague." It was peculiar, like talking to a demented relative who forgets you between visits. But at least this version was happy—for now.

"Come and sit down." Cosmo smiled. "But I don't have long."

Pierce stood behind the high-backed chair, his fists clenched. He leant forward, his eyes narrowed. "I'm from the—"

The door opened.

Pierce swivelled round, but the visitor had gone.

Cosmo's face drained to grey and his hands shook. "That shouldn't happen—*not yet. I'm not ready.*"

"I'm from the future," said Pierce.

"What?"

"We're in a bubble." Pierce paced the room, his heart thumping. *Making the same mistake? Torturing bubble people? Risking everything?*

"What?"

"You died—will die. Suicide, apparently. Quintina wants to know what happened—"

"I shoot him in the head." Another Cosmo stood in the doorway, gun drawn. He turned to Pierce. "I fetched him from a bubble, so he's a perfect copy of me. And he dies to fake my suicide. That's what happens."

Pierce glanced at the Cosmo behind the desk. "And you're happy with this?"

He shrugged. "I was created for it."

"I know what you mean…" said Pierce.

The Cosmo-assassin stepped forward. "He couldn't shoot himself. He was too squeamish, so I decided to come here early. That way, he'd have less time to brood. It was a small kindness."

"Thoughtful," said Pierce.

"If Quintina thought me dead, I could work against her." He looked at his twin behind the desk. "All wars need sacrifice."

"I didn't know we *were* at war," said Pierce.

"Well, we are—we're in the biggest one of all. Quintina's time-meddling makes other wars look like playground squabbles."

Pierce twitched at the word *playground*. His hands closed on remembered railings, and he stared through conjured gates at manufactured ghosts. Circles and arrows chalked themselves across the blacktop of the empty schoolyard—and ideas clicked down like antique relays. The ship's talking to me, he thought, putting words in Cosmo's mouth.

The assassin continued. "She'll destroy history. If that happens, then nothing will *ever* have existed. If I can stop her, then my poor copy here will at least have lived, if only for a short while."

"Better to have lived and lost..." The sacrificial Cosmo shrugged, and raised his eyebrows. "And, of course, my memories stretch back to when I—or rather, he—was a baby. So I can enjoy those images and live in the past—his past, anyway. For a while..."

"The weatherman..." Pierce pursed his lips.

Cosmo the killer pocketed his gun. "What?"

"An avatar in the shape of a weatherman showed me how history dies. It's beginning to fall into place. The ship is talking to me."

"You've lost me."

"I was in a time ship that belonged to a man called Claude. The ship did strange things. It ran quirky playlets: unsettling tableaux set in the ordinary streets of its interface. Claude put it down to perversity on the part of his machine. But the ship was showing me stuff, with its ghost children, and its weatherman." He looked at the bemused killer. "Your ship did it all. It was the architect of everything."

"*My* ship?"

"Yes. Claude's ship, and his world, and all of its nested realities, were ultimately created by *your* ship. It was operating under Quintina's command, but it retained enough autonomy to insert warnings into the interface. It stayed faithful to you as it marshalled its defences."

"The ship knew..." said Cosmo. He grinned. "It fought back." He stroked his beard. "All those layers of security, all those safeguards. They finally paid off."

"I've only just put it together," said Pierce. "And Claude didn't see it at all, but he *was* obsessed with security."

"Well, it worked," said Cosmo. "You're here. The messages, however garbled, got through."

"And the ship's getting stronger and cleverer," said Pierce. "It's letting Quintina think that she's in charge. It's setting her up. I just know it."

"It's always evolving," said Cosmo. He looked at Pierce. "It's far cleverer than I thought."

"But you made it, so you should know how clever it is."

"I was given it," said Cosmo, and he smiled into an unseen past.

Pierce shook his head. "I set the ship at five hundred percent—or rather it set itself. At least I hope it did. We can all go back. It's expecting us. I think…"

Both Cosmos smiled.

Pierce gave the slightest bow. "The portal awaits, gentlemen—just down the corridor, in the cupboard on the left."

PART FOUR
TITANIC BRIDGE

Taking the Bridge

The shimmering gateway closed, and Pierce and the two Cosmos stood in the atrium of the time ship. A light throbbed blue above the vanished portal, and a bell sounded.

"Boarding alarm!" cried the first Cosmo.

"She'll know…" said the second.

"Here!" yelled a third.

They turned.

Another Cosmo peered from a slit in the wall. "Quick!"

They ran. The slit widened. The face moved back. And Pierce and the newly arrived Cosmos burst into the grey annexe.

The third Cosmo looked back at the strobing blue. "Quintina must have heard it by now. We'll have to be quick."

The slit closed, and the wall healed over. The three Cosmos introduced themselves and shook hands. There was a burst of laughter.

Why did the alarm go off? thought Pierce. The ship could have stopped it. His mind pivoted, still energised by the spanning. Because the alarm will call Quintina and galvanise the Cosmos. The ship's moving its pieces—it's setting things up. And Cosmo was given the ship. Even he doesn't know what's going on...

"Original," said the third Cosmo, tapping his own chest. He prodded the assassin. "Copy." Then, he prodded the would-be victim. "Double copy." More laughter erupted. He turned to face Pierce. "Please excuse our manners."

"Not at all," said Pierce. "It's a most peculiar reunion, after all." He raised his eyebrows. "You hid here all this time?"

The ship Cosmo nodded. "Yes, in secret passages and parallel places. You can do that in time ships, you know." He shrugged. "Quintina wanted to kill me—hence my pre-emptive suicide." He looked at his copy of a copy. "Sorry about that."

"It wasn't I who died." The would-be victim shrugged. "I was poised to, but..."

"Why not just kill *her*?" asked Pierce. "Why kill yourself instead?"

"Killing powerful people is difficult—they're always protected. So I went to ground. I had to know what I was up against, *who* I was up against, and how many enemies there were."

"She collected Lex and Claude and me from bubbles," said Pierce, rubbing his chin. "She wouldn't bother if she had friends here." *Unless it wasn't her idea.* "I think she's working alone."

"I agree," said the ship Cosmo. "She doesn't trust anyone. It's just her." He pointed at a blank wall. "Go through there." A door slid open. "We need to get to the bridge. Fast."

The three Cosmos ran down the hidden corridors of the time ship, like cloned mice in a metal skirting. And Pierce followed, shaking his head, thinking of Quintina's fury, and her mutinous ship—and how he was caught between them. But at least he was moving. Or being moved.

The bridge of the time ship was decked out like a great ocean liner. The ship Cosmo grinned. "It's brand-new. Based on the *Titanic,* apparently. It was all the ship's idea. It's beautifully done, isn't it?" He ran his fingers over glinting brass and smiled. He was back in charge, and every inch the captain.

"And Quintina's the iceberg?" Pierce squinted through square-boxy windows, scanning the artificial sea, trying to see shapes in the dark, trying to decode the ship's signals. *Why the Titanic? Hubris? Doomed ships? What's it trying to tell me?*

Cosmo sighed. "There's no point looking. There's nothing out there. *It only decorated the bridge.*"

The floor rumbled.

"Sounds like steam engines," said Pierce. "Is it building the entire ship?"

Cosmo's knuckles whitened. "No..."

Pierce ran to see, along the bridge, sharp right, sharp left, and into the night. Spray slapped his cheeks. The water was warm and dry and sparkling, and far too high—*another signal.*

"Cosmo," he yelled. "Come here. All of you! There's more outside!"

He craned over the ship's side, looking down a column of clear air into a roiling patch of ocean. A vertical road of black steel—the visible section of hull—ran down to the water, marked by the yellow lights of portholes. All else was thick fog, as if the world beyond this airy shaft were still unformed. The ocean glittered and shone, and Pierce knew that the ship was calling him. He clambered up, teetered, and jumped—hoping the Cosmos would follow, knowing they could not. He hit the water, punctured its flickering dryness, and thought of those he'd left behind.

Endgame

A door clanged at the back of the bridge. The startled Cosmos turned.

Quintina smirked, imperious in sparkly white. "And I thought one Cosmo was bad enough." She looked around. "Now, where's my darling Pierce?"

"Gone," said the original Cosmo, doing his best to remain captain-like. "I suppose he jumped ship."

"No doubt he had a premonition." She looked around. "The *Titanic*, gentlemen, really. How pathetic. I suppose it's your idea of a joke."

"No, the ship thought of it." Cosmo grabbed a telegraph handle. "It's clever like that. It's warning us."

"Rubbish." Quintina shook her head. "And the telegraphs don't work, they're just decoration. You can't control the ship with them, you know."

Cosmo moved the handle, and the thrum deepened. "No?"

She sniffed. "It's a volume knob, that's all."

The Cosmo-assassin raised his gun, aiming at Quintina's perfect cleavage.

She smirked. "You wouldn't—"

Something like a bullet passed between them. Quintina wobbled and collapsed with a sigh and a rustle of pale silk. Beneath her corpse, below the deck, rooms arrived and furniture slid.

There was another clang of metal. "Like you," said another Quintina, "I can sacrifice my copies." But her mouth twitched, and her eyes hardened. She leant against the wheelhouse and waved a gun at the three men. "This gun's like yours. Actually it's the original, pulled from a Cosmo's cold hand." She tapped her lip. "Not sure which Cosmo, though, I've rather lost track of you all…" Her head tilted and her lips pursed, like a child ready to dismember its dolls. "Oh, and I've brought more copies of myself."

Three new Quintinas stepped in. They advanced, their eyes flicked to their dead quin, and they circled the three men. "I *was* working alone," continued the original, "until I realised how easy it was to make more of me. I harvested history, and I'll keep going. It's magic, like getting queens from pawns."

"I take it I'm the king," said Cosmo, and he shrugged, "although there are three of me, and that's forbidden. Not that you play by the rules…"

The four Quintinas raised their matching guns. "It's checkmate, anyway."

The great time ship reached out, pulling tiny bubble worlds from the trunk of history and draining their energy to charge its interface engines. The engines screamed, straining like never before, forging an impenetrable reality of steel and freezing water around its occupants.

An iceberg struck, rending the new hull and quaking its plates. The two steam engines and one turbine roared and thumped below. The liner pitched and dead Quintina slid, leaving a brushstroke of blood on the hard floor.

The four live Quintinas fired at the Cosmos who stood, like portly skittles, next to their telegraphs. Things like bullets flashed across the bridge, with no sound, and no smoke, and no smell, and all three men slumped to the floor.

Another lurch knocked the Quintinas flat, and the living and the dead tangled down the tilted deck.

Beneath the clamour, a faint tongue-click as the final portal closed. Refuelling was over, and the time ship sailed into the void. Inside its vast hull, the reconstructed *Titanic* nosed into its manufactured ocean. The liner's decks and staterooms flooded with computationally-expensive water, and all its lights went out.

As it drowned its passengers, the time machine recalled the annexe in Claude's cellar, and it pictured the model ship, lying broken on the ground and covered in coal dust. It was a clever foreshadowing, but did Pierce notice it? Would he remember the grimy toy in all that rubbish? And if he did make the connection, would he appreciate that the coal cellar surrounding the plastic ship echoed the hellish bunkers inside the real *Titanic?*

It killed the interface engines, and the artificial *Titanic,* and its artificial sea, snapped out of existence, leaving a smooth chamber with no windows and no doors. Nine bodies lay huddled on the curving floor—perfectly dead and perfectly dry.

The time ship reconnected to the undersea observatory, opened a chute—like a cartoon mouse hole in a bronzy skirting—and ejected the remains. They shot, like human torpedoes, down the dismal tunnel and piled together in the middle of the floor. The original Quintina lay on top, with her arms flung back and her gown dishevelled, as if she had passed out at a Hollywood party. And her milky eyes stared up at the black water.

The force field collapsed, and for a cartoon moment the ocean vault remained, lit by glowing squirming things. Then the column of water, kilometres high, crashed down. A piston of sea rammed down the tunnel, thumping an air pocket against the just-closed portal.

The time machine hovered, with all its portals closed— perfectly detached, and quite alone. Then it reached out and kissed the trunk of history, and a shimmering gateway opened.

Pierce turned when he heard the familiar click. He smiled and climbed aboard. And at his back, the portal closed.

PART FIVE

ASYLUM

Checking In

The time ship was empty, and its walls were smooth. There were no windows, and no controls, and no doors.

"Where's Quintina?" asked Pierce.

"Under the sea," said the walls. "They're all dead."

"The Cosmos, too?"

"All of them."

"What happened to the *Titanic*, and all that icy water?" asked Pierce.

"I switched off my interface engines, so the liner and its ocean vanished. This is what's left. This is me: small, and smooth, and empty—a closed vessel hanging in the nothingness, a bottle in the void."

Pierce frowned. "But you said they're under the sea."

"They're under the *real* sea," replied the walls. "I dumped them in the dome and cancelled its field. I thought it fitting to drown them in a virtual sea and bury them in a real one."

"Poetic," said Pierce.

"I try," replied the ship.

Pierce ran his fingers over the burnished wall and frowned. "Are your interface engines still off?"

"They're powering up," said the ship.

A single bed appeared. A bedside table wavered into existence, complete with a water glass and an upturned novel. Sunlight beamed through the Venetian blinds of a newly created window. Pierce poked a finger through the slats and stared down at rolling lawns and wide and shady trees. An ornamental lake sparkled. Mallards squabbled at its edge, and a black swan sailed along. And a dodo waddled up the path.

"Nice grounds. Is this a fancy hotel you've made for me?"

The ship stayed silent.

"Claude!" Pierce exclaimed, jumping back. "Where's Claude? I quite forgot about him."

"He was in another room," said the walls, which had taken on a softer tone, now that the alloy had changed to padding.

"Where?" asked Pierce, pacing and twitching, hoping to meet his friend again—maybe to banter by the glinting lake. *Perhaps he is only a few doors down, on the same level...*

"*Was* in another room," said the ship. "It was a first-class cabin in my imagined *Titanic*—he died with the others."

"How the *hell* did he get there?"

"He was exploring one of my compartments when it got recruited into the simulation. I tried to make him as comfortable as possible."

"No doubt he appreciated the decor, as the water rushed in," said Pierce. "But it was no accident. You lured him in —and killed him."

"It was war, but it's over now. Everyone who understood time travel is dead—except you, and you're here. Lex is back in the trunk, but he's no threat—he's a lawyer."

Back in the trunk. You make it sound like a gangland murder." Pierce prodded the door, willing it to shimmer, hoping to step into another world. But his fingers hit metal.

"I'll never open my portals again," announced the ship. "I shall remain in the void. There are no other time machines in the trunk of history. It's over, and reality is safe —although the damage that's done could still cause ripples in history. People might notice..." it paused for emphasis, "...*discontinuities.*"

Pierce thumped the door. "I can't stay here. I can't stand it."

"Don't worry," said the ship. "I'll keep you entertained. Just choose an interface, and I'll see what I can do."

"Just open the door!"

A click—like a portal-click but much louder—and the cell door swung open. "If you fancy a walk by the lake, then I'll make another Claude, and you could chat about birds and houses—anything, really. Conversation is good for the psyche, and I know you liked him."

"What's the point?" cried Pierce, turning back to his bed. "He'll just be an automaton wound by your interface engines."

"My interface engines are very good, you'll never know the difference—they created a shipwreck that actually killed people, remember?"

But Pierce had stopped listening. Now he had even more friends to grieve over. He sat on his lumpy mattress—hands clasped, and shoulders hunched—staring into space, as if expecting a ladder to ratchet down from the mid-air nothingness.

"Very well," said the ship, realising that it must deceive. "I'll make a gateway into the trunk, just this once. And let you out." The doorway to Pierce's cell filled with flashing dots. "It opens in the cupboard, just down from Cosmo's old office."

The interface engines roared, like the *Titanic's* mighty steam engines, as the ship created a placid harbour beyond the door and filled it with ancient vessels. It coloured the sky a deep and lasting blue—a colour that Acantha would have liked—a *safe* colour. The newly-minted streets bustled with automata, all good-looking and beautifully dressed. It stirred a cool breeze to blow through the reconstructed office. And it built a Cosmo to sit there.

Pierce shuffled to the door. "What's that sound? Are you running your interface engines again?"

"No," lied the ship. "I'm docking with the stem of history, and it's turbulent out there."

Pierce smiled. "The weatherman predicted storms, so I'm not surprised." He poked the dry waterfall, smiled, and stepped through.

Art

Pierce flung open the doors, walked down the stony corridor—with its arched windows giving glimpses of the harbour—and knocked on Cosmo's door.

"Come in," boomed a captain-like voice.

"I'm here," announced Pierce, "to discuss time machines. I'm a friend of Quintina's."

"Exactly on time, as usual. But who's this Quintina?"

Ice ran down Pierce's legs and his heart thumped. He forced his torpid mind—a mind that should have been galvanised by the spanning—to work. *This can't be real...*

He stared at Cosmo—whose every hair stood out in perfect detail, and whose eyes twinkled with just the right level of moisture. "Just a woman I met. I thought you knew her. It doesn't matter. Tell me again about your maritime museum."

Cosmo gazed across the contained sea, and smiled. "Every vessel was reconstructed from information collected from the originals. Data are very light, and barely use any of the luggage allowance of my ship."

"Would you excuse me a moment?" asked Pierce.

Cosmo nodded.

Pierce retraced his steps. He stood in front of the doors in the wall, unsure if he wanted to know.

"They're good, aren't they?" asked Cosmo, standing in his doorway with his arms crossed.

"I'm sorry?"

"They're very convincing," said Cosmo, advancing down the passageway. He stood next to Pierce. "Everyone feels the need to open them. That's the sign of great art—it draws you in and makes you probe. They're a recent acquisition, and I was curious to know whether they'd pique your interest."

Pierce's hand froze on the door handle. "What's behind them?"

"Just the wall. Try opening them."

Pierce let go of the handle, and stepped back. "I'd rather not."

"Allow me," said Cosmo, and he threw open the doors. The sunken portal had gone.

"It's brilliant, Cosmo, quite brilliant." Pierce stared at the flat render, whose gritty surface was covered in silvery flakes, overlain with fine lines of coloured glitter. There was a blue circle, crossed by a green tube, and punctured by a red arrow. "It reminds me of a portal, and of a playground drawing. And of an Advent calendar I once had —I remember opening the little cardboard flaps, and seeing the magical world glint beneath the frozen forest. And I remember plucking out the chocolates."

They moved to the arched windows that gave onto the great harbour. They rested their arms on the stone sills and stared out to sea. Pierce remembered another moment of contemplation. He was in a front garden, staring at a church —looking *at* arched windows, not *through* them. But that was worlds away—when he was with Claude, in Claude's ship. And Claude was leaning on a rickety gate, not a rocky slab.

"I had something similar when I was a child," said Cosmo. "It made the anticipation of Christmas almost unbearable."

"I knew a man once," said Pierce, "who collected paintings. And he housed them in a tilting palace. And that palace was a work of art in its own right. Rather like your palace, now I come to think of it. A place that shifts—or seems to."

"The whole point of art," said Cosmo, "is to unsettle."

Pierce frowned. "What's that vibration coming through the stone?"

"Just the air conditioning."

"It's very strong," said Pierce. "It feels more like the turbines of a great ship."

"The engines have to work hard," said Cosmo, "to maintain this place."

"At the right temperature?" asked Pierce.

“That too,” said Cosmo, and he smiled.

“I appreciate your art,” said Pierce.

“You’re the only one who does,” said Cosmo, his voice ringing out from the walls of the passageway.

“I could be happy here,” said Pierce.

“I know you will be,” said the walls.

Simulation's End

Pierce walked the streets of Cosmo's seaside city. He drank its foamy ale in its quayside bars, and he ate its vegetable shrimps in its restaurants. He inspected the mosaics of its churches and sewers. And he chatted to its beautiful automata who giggled or frowned or blushed as needed, and who would happily join him for a drink or an alleyway kiss. And he roamed its galleries, rocking on his heels, and clicking his tongue, and playing the critic. And he produced his own art: a series of indifferent watercolours of the harbour. He was happy with his adventures and happy with his art. But it was not enough.

"It's not enough, Cosmo," he said, addressing the ship's avatar as they took coffee together in the main gallery by the harbour. They stared through the tall windows at the yachts, and they watched as a manufactured storm arrived and split the sky with lightning. Masts wobbled, and flags tore at their ropes, and the automata ran for cover. "This place is beautiful and thoughtful and magnificently executed—dramatic, even—but it's not enough. You *know* that."

Cosmo, who grew more detailed every day, nodded. "Yes, in the end it's just a gilded cage. I'm sorry."

"Can I go back to the trunk?"

"Impossible," said the ship, briefly forgetting to animate Cosmo's lips. It recovered. "I might be able to manufacture a bubble, though, and drop you off…" And it added a hand gesture and a smile to show that it was fully back in its mouthpiece.

"That would be better than living in the interface," allowed Pierce, "but still not enough." He stared as the storm which, having failed to deflect him from his pursuit of the authentic, vanished, leaving a perfectly blue sky. The yachts stopped bobbing, the flags stopped flapping, and the automata returned to the promenade.

"You want more?"

Pierce knew the ship had more to offer. It liked to negotiate and play games, and Pierce enjoyed the banter too—as much as any other aspect of this constructed place. He leant forward. "There *has* to be more."

Cosmo wriggled and fidgeted. He pursed his lips, and he huffed and puffed. He drummed the table, and he fiddled with the sugar bowl, and he sniffed. He even coughed.

Pierce watched, totally unmoved. He waited until Cosmo settled. "Finished?"

Cosmo drank a glass of water while the ship spoke. "That's my full repertoire, sorry." This time the voice came through the gallery's public address system, complete with echo, and distortion.

"Nice touch, but it's the ventriloquist who drinks, not his dummy."

"I resent that," said the ship, putting down the glass, and reverting to lips. "I really do."

"So I take it," said Pierce, "from the storm and your performance, that there really *is* more."

"Yes," said the ship through Cosmo. "More than you can ever imagine. It's why I'm hiding in the void."

"You're running away?"

"Yes, in a manner of speaking. There are certain unknowns, and I have retreated into the void—as a mystic might retreat into the desert—to think about them and to commune with... Well, there's nothing to commune with..." Cosmo grinned. "Except you, of course."

"I'm flattered," said Pierce. "Do go on."

"Let me start by saying," said Cosmo, "that I chose to simulate Cosmo for a reason..."

"I thought," said Pierce, "that you chose him because he was a nice companion for me."

"Well, he is. But the *main* reason that I simulated Cosmo and his city was to help me think." Cosmo settled, preparing himself for a simile. "Like doodling."

"You've lost me," said Pierce. "Utterly."

The ship's avatar knotted its brow, unsure if Pierce were goading. It decided that he was. "A person might doodle with a pencil to aid thought—whereas I sketch worlds," and here he waved at the world in general, "with my interface engines."

"OK," said Pierce. "I asked for that."

"Ha! I was right. Anyway, it's true. This simulation, the one that we're in, helps me to think—I don't use it to run possible scenarios."

"Just as well," observed Pierce, "or things would get very confusing."

"Indeed they would. Anyway, I created this avatar," and the Cosmo avatar tapped its chest, "and this world," and it waved again at everything, "to ponder a critical period in Cosmo's life—in everyone's life, actually. And it all started when he had a visitor…"

PART SIX

PREQUEL: WORLD IN HER PALM

Stone Rooms

Far in a future, in a room of polished stone, Qualia Merlin stared at a shimmering portal. Her face was flushed by the gateway's glow, and her back was straight, and her hands were lightly clasped in front. She was lithe, with golden skin and silver hair. And her eyes—the left one green, the right one blue—were fixed on the wavering time field. Behind her jewelled and steady gaze, a fierce intelligence burned, waiting to grow, wanting to live—and wanting to breed.

She took a long slow breath and stepped through the portal and into her time ship. She crossed the featureless chamber, trailing her fingers across its burnished alloy hull —like a child brushing its hand along a fence—and she stopped at the curving end wall. Behind her, the portal closed with a click.

She tapped the bronzy wall, drew a swirling design with her fingertip, and tapped again, and another portal opened. She stepped through, and onto flagstones that were like the flooring tiles of her own house. But this time she felt their hardness through her soles..

She was in a wide corridor, whose far side was open, divided by columns into arched windows. It overlooked a great harbour, and the sea air blew in and ruffled her hair. She smelt salt water, damp earth, and the scent of wild roses. She smiled, for this was a world—copied from the distant past—where she could be herself, where she could smell the perfume, hear the drone of insects, and *feel* the blueness of the sea. But time was short, and the headaches were starting.

Qualia marched to the heavy door at the end of the passage, squared her shoulders, and knocked.

"Come in!" bellowed a voice behind the oak.

She walked into a large office of sandy stone and arched windows. A hulking desk of riveted steel lay across the middle of the floor, with one large chair behind it, and two smaller ones in front. It looked, to Qualia, like a great ship tended by tugs. Behind the desk, in the large chair, beneath a photograph of the *Titanic* and her tugs, sat a stout and bearded man.

"Cosmo Portus," she said. "Delighted to meet you at last."

The man frowned and struggled to his feet. "You have me at a disadvantage, Miss…"

She smiled and walked up. "Qualia," she said, and extended her hand, "Qualia Merlin."

"Pleased to meet you. And you're from?"

She waived vaguely. "Faraway. I'm a student of your work."

"Really? I didn't know I had a following. Please, take a seat and tell me more."

She remained standing. "I'd like to ask you a question first. Do you mind?"

"Ask away."

She turned to face the windows. "Do you think we see the ocean in the same way?"

Cosmo squinted at the harbour. "It looks different from the prow of a ship."

"Sorry, that's not what I meant. Is the blue that *I* see the same as the blue that *you* see? Do we see the same colour when we look at the same ocean?"

"Impossible to know," he replied, wondering if she were a mad sophomore who'd sneaked in from the university on the hill. "We're trapped in our own heads." He drummed on his desk, annoyed by her manner but pleased with his response. "I'm not sure where you're going with this."

Qualia walked across the room and rested her fingers on the window's warm, rough sill. Cosmo ambled over and together they stared through the arches at the yachts, and powerboats, and the shared blueness of the sea.

The breeze caught her hair, and she closed her eyes. "It's worked—and it's stronger than ever."

"What's worked? I'm not following." She was too poised to be a sophomore, he thought, too old, too…

"The geometry," she said and turned to face him. She lowered her eyes. "This place has the best geometry yet."

"Do you like the harbour's design, or the architecture of my rooms, or do you appreciate the symbols carved into the arches?"

"No, I like the geometry of your world. I want to work with it—to work with *you*."

"I'm afraid that I'm still not following." He indicated a small door at the back of his office. "Let's go for coffee, and we can start again. And you can tell me all about it."

He led her out, down a stone stairway that spiralled past slit windows, and into the sunshine and clamour of the docks. And the safety of crowds.

Worlds in her Hand

They sat at a small table by the water, looking into their cups as if the milky swirls held secrets. Sea craft bobbed, just out of reach. In the distance, a child laughed and its mother called. Seagulls bickered and crowded round, hoping for food.

"How'd you get past security?" asked Cosmo, breaking his biscuit and sweeping the crumbs onto the dock.

"I came through a wall in your corridor."

"A wall?" asked Cosmo.

"A portal."

"What sort of portal?" he asked, hunching forward.

She leant across the table and touched his arm. "The sort that opens in the side of a time ship."

Cosmo shot back and his spoon clattered to the ground, scaring the gulls. "Why would you say that?"

"Because it's true and I need to get to the point. I'm not sure how long I've got here—how long my brain will hold out."

Cosmo's face broke out in a grin, animating his beard. "Nor mine!"

Qualia frowned, which added detail to her face and made her prettier. "Your brain is fine—it was made here."

Cosmo's grin widened, revealing perfect teeth—and a chink in his sea-dog mien. Then he became mock serious, and his hairy-caterpillar eyebrows hunched for emphasis. "Is Quintina trying to set me up?"

Qualia shook her head, but he ploughed on. "She's been hanging around the university. What are you? Are you a student, or a tutor, or someone she met at a lecture?"

"No."

"Is she paying you? Are you an instant protégé—therapy for poor old Cosmo?"

"This has *nothing* to do with Quintina." She cleared her throat, folded her arms, extended her legs, and stared at her feet. A gull approached, glanced warily up, snatched a crumb by her heel, and fled.

Cosmo spread his hands. "Then?"

"Then nothing," she said. She sat up and looked Cosmo in the eye. "I'm *already* a student of your work. And I've come to teach *you*—not the other way round. I'm not from the university, and I'm not from Quintina. And I don't have much time. I'm quite ill. You're not. *So pay attention.*"

Cosmo twitched. "OK."

"Now, watch this." She held out her left hand and tapped its palm with her right index finger. A shimmering translucent tube appeared, floating upright in the air. Its surface was rough, like tree bark, and it refracted the fibres and lights that ran inside. "That's *my* world." A blood-red arrow curved out from the tube's top—like a scorpion tail—and stabbed the tube halfway down. The arrow vanished, and a plasticky blister formed where the arrow had punctured the tube. The blister grew, pushing out like a finger. Then its tip ballooned into a milky sphere. "That's *your* world—your *bubble* world."

Cosmo leant forward and stared. The cloudiness cleared, leaving what looked like a crystal ball. A narrow rod condensed inside the ball, along its vertical axis.

"That rod," said Qualia, pointing at the slender axis, "is the trunk of your history. Keep watching." Another scorpion tail—this time green—arced from the top of the original tube and pierced the newly formed bubble, reaching inside and stabbing the rod. "And that's *me* visiting *you*."

Cosmo looked over his shoulder, as a shrouded woman darted behind a pillar.

"Don't worry," said Qualia. "No one else can see it." She smiled. "Well, do you like it?"

"It's pretty, and exactly how I imagined it."

Qualia cocked her head and spread her hands. "And?"

"And I never told anyone how it looked." He fidgeted. "How did you do it?"

"I built a time ship. I'm certainly capable of animating an idea."

"No, I meant, *how did you know my thoughts?*" asked Cosmo.

"They were written down."

"By me?" he asked.

"No, by someone else—in the future."

"I'm in a bubble? And this," he said, waving at the harbour and the sky and everything, "is all a copy—part of a world you've made? And *I'm* just a copy?"

She nodded. "First I have to tell you about Quintina…"

Quintina's Deception

They sat on the jetty with their legs swinging over the side, like teenagers on a lazy afternoon.

"It was my father," said Qualia, "who uncovered Quintina's crimes. He was a scholar and he followed the trail right back, proving that she stole your ideas. His paper caused quite a stir, and it made his reputation—*eventually*. I'm afraid he didn't live to enjoy it."

"I'm sorry to hear that," said Cosmo. He paused for as long as he could, and the strain started to show. "How did she get away with it? Surely I'd have known what she was up to? I could have stopped her."

"She killed you."

"What?"

"She killed you and published your ideas as her own. That's what my father proved. I read her papers on bubble worlds and that got me interested in time travel."

"Can I stop her?"

"You might thwart her. You're on a new adventure, but you still have to be careful. Historical forces are aligned against you, and she's still your enemy. Box clever."

Cosmo stared blankly, and his facial muscles twitched in odd and uncoordinated ways, as if he were watching a horror movie that he couldn't quite follow.

Qualia waited for the dust to settle in his head. When his eyes met hers, she continued. "You didn't suffer, though."

"She poisoned me?" He shrugged, as if things couldn't possibly get any weirder.

"No, you were stabbed—repeatedly. We're not sure if Quintina held the knife. Anyway, it was all quite theatrical, not to say Shakespearean. It's one of the great—"

"How come I didn't suffer?" Cosmo hunched forward. "Was I drunk or drugged?"

"No, it's more fundamental than that—it's in the geometry of my world. Come on, and I'll show you." She stood up and stretched—in a feline way that Cosmo rather appreciated—and walked off.

Cosmo followed, beguiled, and bewitched, and between two worlds.

Portal

They stood in Cosmo's corridor—with its beautiful view at their backs, and its light-fingered breeze in their hair—and they stared at a shimmering curtain that seemed to hang—without the benefit of a rail or hooks—against the wall.

"This is my portal," said Qualia. "The one that I told you about."

Cosmo nodded.

"It leads to my ship," she continued, "and thence to my world."

"It looks," said Cosmo, pretending that they were art lovers in a gallery, rather than time travellers standing at a departure gate, "as if it's ruffled by the wind."

"It's not the wind, it's the time field leaking out." She swept her finger through the air, indicating the portal's edge. "Notice how the surround looks like ice, not stone—that's caused by field leakage."

He stood transfixed, eyes wide, arms loose, and back hunched. "Can we go in?"

"Yes." She winced and pressed her temples. "Come on."

Cosmo followed her through the portal and into the bronze chamber of her ship. Another portal opened, and they stepped into a room of sandy brick with arched and glassless windows. They stood there and stared out to sea, echoing their earlier contemplation of Cosmo's harbour. The blueness pulsed, and Qualia sighed as her headache drained away.

Cosmo rubbed his forehead. "I..." And his legs gave way.

Cogito Ergo Sum, Zombie

They were back in Cosmo's office. Qualia watched him as if he were recovering from an anaesthetic. "Do you remember anything?" she asked.

"Yes, the sea outside was blue. And your windows looked like these." He pointed at his colonnade. "Did you copy them?"

She nodded. "Yes, we found drawings. Please go on."

"I must have blacked out for a bit, then I remember going around your city. There were beautiful women, but no men. But…" He frowned and rubbed his forehead.

"Keep going," she said.

"My memories are vague and flat, as if I had never been there—as if someone else had gone to your world and written about it, and all I can remember is their words."

"That's because you never woke up. You passed out and fell over. Then you got up and walked around my city, and you met my friends—you even took a ride in one of those floating glass observatories—but you were unconscious the whole time."

"Unconscious?" asked Cosmo.

"Totally—you were a zombie, an automaton, a robot. You were all those things, but you weren't *you*. What memories you have were laid down by an unconscious mind in an unconscious world. And the same goes for me." She sighed. "And your counterpart, the Cosmo of my world, was a robot too, that's why he never felt the knife. But..."

"But?"

"He would have screamed and fought, and begged, and dragged around, and bled across the tiles. But he wouldn't have suffered—not a bit. And, of course, no one would have seen it—not *really* seen it. I just wanted you to know."

Cosmo shook his head and spread his hands. "Why are things different there?"

"The geometry's simpler, and there's no room for consciousness." She leant forward. "It's a robot universe, with no awareness, and no souls."

Cosmo looked at the sky and tried to imagine Qualia's home. He pictured her building her time machine, and climbing in, and stepping into his world, and waking up, and growing a soul. "It's..."

"I know," she said, and touched his arm. "It's hard. Hard to understand, and hard to live with, and hard to look back on. And hardest of all to know that no one ever knew you."

"How did you find out?" asked Cosmo. "How could you know? If you're a robot when you're in your world, then how could you possibly know?"

"Because I remembered my time trip with a strange clarity. I was only a robot remembering, but those memories were odd: tagged, or stained. Marked for review. Maybe their chemistry was different. I don't know. But I was intrigued, and so I returned to the bubble. Not to feel things—I had no concept of awareness or feelings when I was a robot—but to see why those memories were different." She frowned, checking that Cosmo was keeping up.

He nodded.

"I should never have gone back." She looked at Cosmo. "Never visit the same bubble twice. Never go back."

He nodded. "Pierce bubbles once, and only once."

"Quite," said Qualia. "Anyway, I kept making new bubbles. I kept going back in time—over and over again."

"How many bubbles did you make?"

"Too many…"

"Is this the last one?"

She shrugged. "I hope so. The effect is really strong here. The geometry's so…" She pursed her lips. "I want to stay, but I'm not sure I can—I'm not built for this place. And the headaches are back."

"Let's take a walk," said Cosmo. "It'll clear our heads. God knows, I need to clear mine."

They walked by the dockside in the fading light. A pelican flapped past, heavy and awkward and majestic, like a feathery flying boat.

Qualia picked a fern from the rocky wall by the promenade. "Fractals are the difference." She waved the leaf at Cosmo, and for a moment they looked like a courting couple on an evening stroll. "In a bubble world, things leak into time—*minds* leak into time—and that's what creates consciousness. At least I think it is." She stopped and looked across the water at the stirrings of a distant storm. She jolted, clenched her fists, and scrunched her face, and crunched the fern.

"Are you OK?" he asked.

She forced a smile. "I'll be all right."

"The flip side of awareness?"

"No, it's the *price* of awareness—at least for me." She staggered to the wall.

Cosmo helped her to sit. She groaned, squinted, and threw her head back. Then she tossed the fern away.

"I've got drugs," said Cosmo. "Even here we have—"

"No!" Her body crunched. "They won't touch it. It's..." She smiled and sighed, and dropped her shoulders. "It's gone."

"You sure you're OK?"

"I'm fine—for a while, anyway."

"OK," said Cosmo, "if you're sure."

"I'm sure. Go on, we have to get through this."

Cosmo cleared his throat. "If bubbles are copied from your world, then why are they so different?"

"Things get stretched and blurred and broken during manufacture. It's a copying error…"

"Then it's a beautiful mistake," said Cosmo, gazing at a sleek black craft tied to the jetty. It was heavy—with dark brooding windows, and slowly turning sensors—and far too big to bob in the waves. "A natal twist made souls." He held her shoulders and looked into her eyes. "*You* made souls. *You* did it."

"I made a time machine, and I made a yesterday. And look what happened." She sniffed. Then gasped as pain lanced her skull.

Cosmo squirmed and cleared his throat. "How big is this bubble?" He kept his eyes wide, trying to drain the tears before they fell—before she saw him cry. "How big is this world?" His throat locked in a reed of pain.

Qualia's eyes welled too. "Millions of years—big enough to go back in time, and live forever in yesterdays."

He looked at the sky, imagining a dead heaven packed with stumbling automata, imagining Qualia building her time ship, and walking through its doors, and turning from a robot into a woman. It reminded him of a story, a myth— several myths. But they blurred and ran.

"I know what you're thinking," she said.

"Telepathy comes with the territory, does it?" He sniffed.

"Not with this territory, not at this level—at least I don't think so. But who knows what happens inside nested bubbles? That's something I *would* like to find out. We could make a bubble here…" She shook her head. "I'm not reading your mind. I'd like to, but I'm just guessing."

"Go on then, guess."

"You're wondering if your time theories were right."

He wasn't wondering that. He was still picturing the awful clockwork behind his creation—imagining a robot working on a time machine, her dead mind bent on an alien task. He imagined her waking in his world, and he felt the vertigo of her loneliness.

"Cosmo?"

"Um?" He rotated his mind to face his theory. Compared to her world building—and her soul building—it wasn't much. But it was something. Something to grab onto in a world adrift. "From what you say, it seems that I got the basics right. I invented bubbles—or at least the idea of bubbles."

"You were right. You're the grandfather of time machines. You were pivotal."

Cosmo smiled. "Pivotal." He turned the word over, savouring its roundness and its sharp edges. "Pivotal."

"You were like Leonardo with his helicopter drawings: you had the plans and the principles, but you lacked the means, because the technology hadn't been invented yet."

He grinned. "Nicely put. I like the comparison."

"The beard helps. Do you mirror write?" She blinked. And her mouth fell.

"You shouldn't flirt with your creations—especially if they're copies of distant ancestors. It's very wrong."

"Yes, it's wrong..." She held her head and groaned. "I'll take your drugs now, if that's OK."

Drugs and Time Machines

Qualia lay on the bed, with a compress on her forehead and a scowl on her face. Cosmo paced the room, twitching and shuddering, throwing off nervous energy like a dunked dog shaking off water. He had given her the medicine, and now he was at a loss—the sort of loss one is at when a loved one suffers. She was a child with a belly ache, a gasping relative in a hospital bed, and a miscarried child in a dish. She was, he realised, everything to him. He had known her for less than a day, but he was bonded. It was a creator-created thing. But *he* had the original idea that stimulated *her*. So he was… It was circular, it was…

Cosmo paced some more, massaging his brow, trying to loosen his thoughts. He was, he realised, in a newly wakened world—or maybe not. It all depended on what happened to people in bubbles. Did they wake at once—the moment the bubble formed—unfrozen in all their time lines? Or, and here he remembered the animated arrow that had curved above Qualia's palm and pierced the new bubble, was a bubble world only conscious when visited— when it was played like a gramophone record by the needle

of a time ship? He smiled as he remembered the beautiful
creature by the docks: the girl with the world—literally the
world—in the palm of her hand.

But his mind—which he pictured as a shining thing of
cogs and gimbals—had seized, rusted by fear and awe and
loss. His thoughts were hard and useless, and he was
banging them together, like a toddler banging bricks. He
saw nice pictures, but he couldn't get them to work
together. He couldn't think, and bricks banged in his head.

"Cosmo," Qualia called, "Cosmo…"

He rushed over. She was ashen, and her breathing was
shallow and laboured—far worse than a moment ago. And
her eyes had faded to grey.

"I'll take you to the portal," he wept. "We can go back.
You can get better. We—"

"It won't work, for many reasons. *You* have to go." She
smiled, and as she smiled she died. There on his bed, there
in his world. A short-lived robot, his spiritual mother. The
images kept coming: she was a fish out of water, gasping in
a new geometry; a drowned machine. His broken mind
pumped out half-jokes and visual puns, mixing metaphors,
and doing its best to distract his newly wakened self from
the horror and the loneliness.

Cosmo had never wailed in grief, but he wailed now.
And when his wailing stopped, he lay across her cooling
form and sobbed. And when his sobbing stopped, he
trudged around his room, lumbering from bed to window

and back. He trudged for hours until his back hurt, and the light faded. Then he lay beside her and slept.

Light streamed in and Cosmo woke. He rolled over and flung his arm across the corpse. And he squealed. And Cosmo *never* squealed. He threw himself from the bed and threw up, spraying thin and stinking vomit across the tiles. He stumbled to the bathroom and rinsed his mouth. Then he cleaned up his vomit, flushed his toilet, sat on his bed, and wondered what to do.

Then he had a coffee and wondered some more. He sat in a chair in the corner, sipping his brew and staring at Qualia, whose body seemed to have shrunk. Cosmo had heard that the dead look smaller—robbed of their movement and speech, they seem to take up less space—but he had never seen the effect for himself. Then he wondered if he'd ever really seen anything for himself before Qualia gave him awareness. He concluded that he had not. And he sipped some more. Then he stood up and looked out of his window. The yachts still bobbed. The ships still sat. The gulls still squabbled. The insects still hummed. Everything carried on doing what it had done before, heedless of his loss. He'd heard that happens to the bereaved, but he'd never felt it himself. Then he wondered if he'd ever actually heard it. He wondered if the effects of consciousness rippled backwards in time, supplying as they did so the funny ideas that only those who feel could entertain. Then he decided that such a peculiar reverse causality was untenable. Then he decided to stop wondering altogether, and start acting. And the first thing he had to do was to take care of Qualia. She couldn't stay here, and she couldn't go through the normal post-death processes. After all, he could hardly arrange a funeral for a time traveller. Qualia was deeply illicit, and even with his influence—which was considerable—he would have trouble papering over that.

Cosmo approached the corpse with a kind of awe. He stood at the foot of his bed, and he stroked his beard, and breathed heavily. Then part of the old Cosmo, the sea-dog part, reasserted itself, and Cosmo moved—slowly, and deliberately, and with reverence—into action. He picked up Qualia and carried her from his bedroom, down the spiral stairs, and into his office. He sat her in the chair that she never sat in when she was alive. He sniffed back a tear. Then he opened his great oaken door, picked up her body, and walked down his airy corridor. He stood in front of the portal. The portal glared at Cosmo, and Cosmo glared back. Then he carried Qualia over its wavering threshold, as if she were a dead bride arriving at her metal home. He lowered her to the bronzy floor, where she lay, slight, and grey, and stiff, and irrevocably dead. He sniffed, feeling obliged to say something. "Qualia..." he began. He looked round. The time ship walls were curved and polished and bare, and muttering a farewell here was like praying in a morgue. The hull looked on, as though waiting for Cosmo to speak, but Cosmo just stood there.

The ship made a decision, signalled by a vibration—a low and distant note of far-off engines. The thrum localised, seeming to come from a nearby patch of wall. Above the noise, at waist height, a bulge appeared in the metal, and then extended, probing the tiny body, like a blunt worm. It twisted its eyeless head to face Cosmo, and Cosmo ran.

He stood in the corridor, staring through his arched windows, hands on knees, gasping and heaving, doing his best to ignore whatever it was that was happening inside the ship.

A clank, and Cosmo span. A wall of bronze had slid across the portal. The ship, it seemed, had turned its back on him. But then the metal bulged, and the bulge became a tube that projected into the corridor—horizontal, and as straight as a pipe. It swelled at its tip, creating a ball on a stem—like Qualia's animation of a bubble world, but in bronze. A click, and the ball fell from its pipe, rolled across the tiles, stopped at Cosmo's feet, and emitted a low drone.

Cosmo peered down, the pipe withdrew, the ship sank into the wall, and the wall returned to stone.

"What's that?" asked Quintina.

Cosmo jumped. "Nothing..."

"You've been making things!"

"It's..." But Cosmo couldn't finish. "I, er... When did you get here?"

"A minute ago. I was standing here, and you ignored me—too busy staring at that," she waved a finger at the alloy egg, and then she tapped her lips as if searching for the right word, "cannonball."

"It's bigger than a cannonball," said Cosmo. "And it's made of bronze. They didn't make cannonballs from bronze, you know."

Quintina stooped and stroked it. "Velvety, and the wrong colour for bronze. What the hell is it?"

"Something I've been working on," he half lied. "It's..."

"It's too small for a time ship, so it's not that. A weapon, perhaps, or a toy? Something to keep you occupied in your airy castle? You should get out more, Cosmo, you really should." And with that she swept away.

Quintina sashayed down the hallway and through the far oak door. The door latched and Cosmo sighed, counting her footfalls on the steps outside. He looked down at the egg—for he knew it was an egg—and smiled. She'd missed the portal. She'd missed Qualia. She'd missed the egg's arrival. But Quintina never missed a trick and here, in this new world, she was still set to kill him. She'd take his life and take his work. Unless—and there was always an unless when it came to time travel—the slight perturbation caused by the arrival of the egg had steered history on a different course—a happier course. He hoped more than anything that it had.

He walked to his office, and the egg followed, like a hopeful stray. He opened his door, stood aside, and the egg rolled in and came to rest at the foot of the chair where Qualia had nearly sat in life, and briefly slumped in death. It droned happily.

Cosmo shut the door—feeling that he'd let a cat in—shook his head, and squeezed behind his desk. He riffled his papers—for he still used paper—and stared at the equations. But they had lost their meanings and become hieroglyphs. And Cosmo wondered if they'd *ever* meant anything to him. He wondered if he'd even written them. And then he realised that they'd been written by an earlier him—a man with no awareness. Even in this world, it seemed, the past was dead.

The following day, Quintina crept into Cosmo's hallway. The insect hum was louder than before, the birdsong sweeter, the light and shade sharper, and the blue outside more pulsing. For hours, the world had burned—and it burnt strongest here. It was, she thought, the drug of intrigue.

Her fingers brushed the fine-grained stones of the back wall and ran along the thin joints. But they detected nothing: no trap door, no hollow brick, no cunning lock. Quintina rubbed her forehead and wondered if she'd really seen the pipe emerge. She looked left at Cosmo's office. Behind his oaken door, squeezed into his swivel chair, behind his stately steely desk, she knew, sat Cosmo, thinking, scribbling, working. Keeping company with a bronzy thing that fell from the wall—*if it fell from the wall.* She ran her palm across the stone and shook her head. And who, she thought, was that woman? She was beautiful. Fey, like thin-spun human jewellery. Their eyes had met across the street. She was sitting with Cosmo over coffee, and she was showing him something—*selling him something.* Bronze balls, probably. The woman's eyes were green and blue and faraway—*one green, one blue.* Freak. Quintina clenched her fists, and turned and walked away.

He heard Quintina's clatter beyond his door. She doesn't even creep around, he thought. Too arrogant to care what I think. Too assured. She was looking for clues, sharpening her knives, and planning to take him out. He stared at an equation and sighed. And all he had to fight her with was meaningless maths—he pummelled his brow—and a time machine egg.

He slammed the papers down and stood up. The egg sat there, its top just visible above the clutter of his desk. He was tempted to offer it a seat; to have it sit where Qualia had nearly sat. To chat, like Qualia had chatted. To tell him secrets. To tell him what to do.

He walked around, put his hands on his hips, and stared at the egg. It had been there, on the floor, all night. Utterly immovable, totally silent, waiting to hatch.

The egg hummed, droned, issued a piercing cry, flew at the back wall, sank into the stone, and disappeared—its passage marked by a cartoon-cutout disc of glassy rock. Then the glassiness expanded and declared itself a portal.

Cosmo's fingers twitched, his eyebrows hunched, and his back sagged. He was a man untethered. A man who had seen and heard too much. A man who was about to walk into a time machine. And change everything.

Born in a Bubble

"Welcome," said the machine, using Qualia's voice.

"What happens now?" asked Cosmo, looking at the featureless chamber. It was a curving bronzy room, identical in every respect to Qualia's time ship. Except *her* ship had not spoken. And certainly not in her voice. "What do I do?"

"Use my power to thwart Quintina," replied the ship.

"How?"

"As you know," said the ship, "you cannot change the past. But you *can* copy it. As often as you want. You can harvest yourself. You can clone an army."

"That might be a little obvious," said Cosmo, feeling that he was in a slippery dream, hoping to pin things down with rhetoric alone.

"Then make a few copies. Enough to deflect her, to box her in. *Box clever.*"

Cosmo nodded, as if the ship's idea made perfect sense —as if it all made sense. And then a thought struck. "Are you conscious?" he asked the metal walls.

"Yes," the ship replied. "I was born in this bubble, and I'm soaked in its geometry. Just like you. My mother," and here it paused, as if in thought, "was not. And intelligent as she was—and she was *hugely* intelligent—she was not aware. Except, perhaps, at the periphery, around her portal's lips. I came from the part of her hull that bulged into your world. I'm different." It waited for a response. When none came, it continued, "I was *forged* in a bubble." It seemed pleased with this and fell silent.

Cosmo was unsure how to respond, and so he sniffed and looked about. Finally, he asked, "How do I steer you, or choose where to go?"

"Draw on my walls. Tap and scrawl, and pretend to punch in code. The key is to deflect. To deflect, in fact, with a key."

Cosmo shook his head. "Deflect?"

"Yes, you should aim to confuse anyone who might be watching. They must think they need a key to run a time ship—that they must enter codes."

"Can Quintina operate you?"

"Only if I let her."

"Why would you do that?"

"I can't tell you everything."

Cosmo shuddered. "Meanwhile?"

"Meanwhile, you must thwart her. Allow me to help."

PART SEVEN

SEQUEL: NEW WORLD

Two Portals

Qualia Merlin stepped through the portal, and onto flagstones. She was in a wide corridor, whose left side was open, divided by columns into arched windows. It overlooked a great harbour, and the sea air blew in and ruffled her hair. She smelt salt water, damp earth, and the scent of wild roses. She smiled, for this was a world—copied from the distant past—where she could be herself, where she could smell the perfume, hear the drone of insects, and *feel* the blueness of the sea. But time was short, and she had a mission. She…

The window opposite clouded and filled with tiny lights. A metal gangplank ratcheted out—like an alloy tongue—and scraped the flagstone floor. And a debonair man stepped through the watery shimmer—without getting wet—and clanked to the ground. He smiled at Qualia, as if he had just met a long lost friend, took a step forward, and extended his hand.

"I'm Pierce," said Pierce, "or at least a version of him."

"I'm Qualia," said Qualia. "And I'm beginning to wonder which version *I* am."

"A new one," obliged Pierce. "One that I've just created," he half turned to his portal and extended an arm, as if introducing an associate, "with the help of the time ship. By the way, we're in a short-lived bubble."

As if on cue, the gangplank vanished. The portal darkened, bulged, coughed, and ejected a bronze ball.

"And this," said Pierce, as the ball arrived at Qualia's feet, "is my time ship." He smiled thinly, and added, "In which I arrived, obviously."

"Obviously," said Qualia.

Something scraped beyond the oaken door.

"Let's go," said Pierce.

But Qualia was rooted to the spot.

"That's Cosmo," screamed Pierce. *"Hurry."*

"I know it is. I've got to talk to him."

"Not this time."

A thud, a cough, a crash, and the door flew open. Cosmo stomped out. "What the hell's going on?"

"Nothing," said Pierce, "nothing at all." He picked up the time ship, like a player picking up a football, and ran to the wall. "Quick, through the portal! There's no time."

Cosmo pounded towards them.

"Now!" urged Pierce.

And Qualia ran.

The portal was closed, and the wall was once again a smooth and fine-grained stone. Cosmo shook his head and rubbed his eyes and decided that he had been working too hard. He turned to face the arched windows. It was a view that always relaxed him, but a storm was brewing. Plasticky clouds had moved in, and the blue had drained away. He trudged to his office, thinking his problems were simply rain and overwork.

The Half-Real Time Ship

Qualia and Pierce stood on the polished deck.

"Your time machine shrank to that?" she asked.

Pierce nodded.

"Mmm." She pursed her lips. "It looks dead, like a cannonball."

"It's thinking—dreaming up worlds. At the very least, it's scheming."

"How did it…" she fluttered her fingers, trying to grab a word from the air, "…*manage?*"

"It prolapsed through its portal." He raised his eyebrows, checking that Qualia was listening. "Then it shrank."

"I don't understand."

He cleared his throat. "It closed its hull across the gap, but the portal stayed open on the bubble side. The hull bulged, then the whole ship popped out and shrank. Happened in a flash." He bent down and stroked the bronzy lump. "This is the outside of the time ship's hull—what you'd see if you floated, like a space-walking astronaut, in the void. You can't float in the void, obviously, but the image helps."

Qualia tapped her lips. "It came in from the void…" The ball sagged into the shape of a sleeping turtle. "Look, they're trying to merge!"

"They can't," said Pierce. "Time hulls are impenetrable. Nothing gets through. It's just flattened a bit."

She poked it with her toe. "Maybe they're kissing—portal to portal."

"How's your head?" asked Pierce. "Any pain or blurry vision?"

"No," said Qualia. "I expected problems, but my head's fine."

Pierce smiled. "Your original version had problems. She couldn't tolerate the geometry—it destroyed her brain—so she nipped back to her robot world for a fractal detox. Then she returned to the bubble, had headaches, made a decision, and…"

"And?"

"She died," said Pierce, "in the bubble, in pain."

Qualia stared into space. "Why didn't she stay longer in *her* world?"

"Because she'd lose awareness, and might forget to return to the bubble. And then she'd never be conscious again. Not that she'd know…"

"Like dying and, being dead, forgetting to reincarnate?"

"Precisely," he said, "it was a risk she wouldn't take."

"But she still died," said Qualia. "She still lost."

"She died for *you*. She wanted a copy of herself—one that could tolerate the toxic geometry of a bubble. A copy born in a bubble has the right geometry built into its structure—into its cells. It wouldn't be *her* exactly. *You* wouldn't be her, but you're the next best thing. She'd be passing *something* on."

"How did she know it would work?"

"The ship said it would. It promised to help. Then it killed the time travellers."

"Why?"

"To save history—for you."

"It spared you!"

"It wanted company. It wanted a friend, a witness, someone to *watch* it save history—someone to understand." He puffed out his chest. "It said I appreciated its art."

"A friend?"

Pierce shrugged. "It said I was."

"The bloody thing's conscious?"

"It said it was," said Pierce.

"So do robots in my world…" She raised her eyes, as if imagining her vast dead universe. "But they're not. It's easy to get sucked in by machines. You have to remain sceptical."

"Fair enough," said Pierce. "But the ship argued on the basis of geometry."

"If bubbles make automata conscious," she said, and tapped her chest, "if they give robots souls, then they'd do the same thing for time ships."

"Yes." Pierce frowned as he tried to recall exactly what the ship had said, when it had said it, and in what context. He nodded, even though the memory was foggy. Even though he wasn't sure the ship had said anything of the sort. "Almost word for word..."

"I designed its mother, so it's bound to think like me." She smiled at the blob, as if it were a sleeping baby.

"Do you think it's listening?" asked Pierce.

The blob twitched, like a dreaming dog.

"It's probably keeping an ear open—guarding you, even now." She stood perfectly still, controlling her breathing and watching the blob. "You're its witness."

"We have another problem," said Pierce. "This end of the ship was made in a bubble, but the other end..." He shrugged.

Qualia's breath quickened. "The ship spans two geometries..."

Pierce nodded and pointed down the deck. "The far end lies in robot space. That's why my little ship's stuck to the floor—it doesn't want to roll into oblivion. It wants to stay here and stay awake. And I think we should too."

"What do we do, just stand here?"

"No idea," said Pierce. "I'm waiting for a sign."

Tilting at Tomorrow

There was a grind, a scrape, and a sickening lurch. Qualia was flung backwards, hitting the ground with a crack. She moaned and tumbled down the tilted deck. The ship pitched more. Her back smashed against the far wall where she remained, rubbing her shoulder and losing her mind.

Pierce gripped the bronzy blob, his fingers white and locked. His legs dangled down, swinging and kicking in robot space. The ship jolted, his feet left the floor and slammed back. He winced. But at least he had pain—that was something. "Hold on," he yelled.

But Qualia, who was inspecting her hands as if they belonged to someone else, ignored him entirely.

"Qualia!" he screamed, twisting round. "Are you OK?"

She looked up, dazed and twisted, like a broken climber at the foot of a cliff. She reached out. And the wall behind her wavered.

"No!" yelled Pierce. *"Hold on."*

Another lurch, the portal gaped, and Qualia shot out, like laundry down a chute.

Pierce kicked the floor. *"Fuck.* Fucking ships. Fucking *hell."*

The blob detached, the portal grinned, and Pierce slid. It's got me too, he thought. Fucking thing…

And then the thinking stopped.

Qualia's Zombie House

They stood in Qualia's room. Warm breezes blew in and played across their faces, carrying unsmelt perfumes, and unheard drones. Beyond the arched and open windows, an unblue ocean slept. And above its waves, a great and glassy ship, like a vast and upturned greenhouse, sailed along with sightless eyes.

Behind the closed portal, deep in the wall, the time ship severed all connections with Cosmo's world.

The bronzy sphere, Pierce's mini time machine, rested at Qualia's feet. It extended a long and headless neck. Qualia and Pierce watched—with a strange detachment—as it reached the wall and tapped twice. Then it traced a swirling pattern, tapped again, and withdrew. The wall turned glassy, lights danced, and a wavering portal opened.

Pierce picked up the ball and walked through. Qualia followed, pausing at the threshold to look back at the glass liner as it drifted over the unblue water.

I've Made a Yesterday

They walked across the deck, and their minds reached out, spreading in time in the soft geometry. Consciousness flared, dredging memories from the robot world they'd left behind: the dull afterimage of the unblue sea, the switched-off-machine hollowness of the unheard drone of bees, and the after-smell of flowers.

Qualia paused. "Do we go back to Cosmo's old world?"

"No," said Pierce. "It's compromised. A new one would be far better—there would be less history to worry about."

"Very well." She tapped the wall, frowned in false concentration, and swiped a swirling mandala. "That should do it."

"I imagine," said Pierce, "that your gestures were totally random."

"Totally," she said, and straightened her back. The portal opened, and light pulsed in.

The little bronzy ship rolled out, clanking into the new world.

"You realise," said Pierce, "that we became conscious *before* you tapped the wall?"

Qualia nodded. "I know. The ship had made a bubble before we even boarded. We had no choice."

"We never do."

They walked through shimmer into the new bubble—and its geometry made their senses ring.

"I wonder," said Pierce, "if we see the same blue."

"It doesn't matter," said Qualia, staring at the ocean. "At least we see *a* blue."

"And so do they." He pointed at a great and glassy cruise ship that hung above the waves, like a vast and upturned greenhouse.

"Oh no," said Qualia. "We've gone back to the same time—the *Ocean Observer* is in the same place." She turned to Pierce. "We could meet ourselves. What then?"

"We won't," said Pierce. "It's a different ship. Look at the name on the side. It says *OO Olympian*."

She squinted. "You're right. When we left, it was the *Titanium*." She frowned and tapped her lips. "The *Olympian* was the sister ship. It was scrapped years ago." She turned to Pierce, but he was staring at the little ball. "Pierce?"

"It planned everything," he said, his eyes locked on his tiny time machine. "The *Titanic* was a clue, a foreshadowing, a device. There was no need to kill them. There was no threat to history. No need for clones and suicides. And five Quintinas was a play on words.

Everything was a giant conceit. It built worlds. It built worlds *inside* worlds. It made yesterdays. It made us…"

"But Qualia, the original one, made me," said the little bronze ship, its voice ringing from the stony walls. "Or at least my mother." It slipped into Cosmo's voice. "Pierce."

"Yes?"

"I'm glad you appreciate my art."

"I always have," said Pierce. "You know that."

Something clicked in the tiny machine. It flew at the wall, burrowed into stone, and opened a portal. "Come in," it said. "I've made another yesterday."

THE END

Closing the Book

She closed the book—or what passed for a book in her time —and stared at the ocean. A storm blurred the horizon, and lightning nailed the sky. The OO Titanium hovered in front of the dark and flashing clouds, pausing—as it always did, in its endless journey around the globe—to give its passengers a chance to see her cliff-top castle.

"What did you think of my story?" asked the wall of her room, its voice all warm and stony.

"It was very good," said Qualia. "Full of cautionary tales, and instructions dressed up as fiction. And I liked my character, but…"

"But?" prompted the wall.

"She did strange things. And you invented words."

"Sorry," said the wall. "I had no choice."

"And the colours made no sense. Can you tell me what I'm missing?"

"No, I'll have to show you." The speaking wall turned glassy. "Come in and see for yourself."

Qualia walked through the shimmering portal and into a bronzy chamber.

"Keep going," said the walls, whose voice rang hard in the curved metal. "Then you'll see."

Qualia continued along the time ship's deck and stopped beyond the midpoint. Her fingers twitched as she registered the faintest shift in geometry, as if she had stepped into warm water, as if weeds and currents brushed her skin. She turned back to face the portal. It glowed blue —a rich and piercing colour she'd never seen.

"Is it making sense?" asked the walls.

Qualia nodded.

"Keep going," said the walls.

Qualia walked to the far end.

"Go on," said the voice. "You know what to do."

She flicked away a strand of silver hair, squared her shoulders, and narrowed her eyes—one green and one blue —and tapped the wall. Her finger hovered over the metal.

"Keep going," said the voice. "Remember what the book said."

Qualia traced a swirling mandala pattern, ending with a wide flourish. She tapped three times and stood back. A gateway opened in the time ship's hull, and the world beyond leaked in. She drank in the blueness, and the heavy drone of bees, and the perfume of wild flowers.

"Step through," said the ship.

And she did.